Other 1632 Universe Publications

1632 by Eric Flint created this universe. Free download available at Baen .com/1632.html. All listed books available at Baen.com.

Short-List of Titles to Jump into the Series:

Ring of Fire anthology edited by Eric Flint

1633 by Eric Flint and David Weber

1634: The Baltic War by Eric Flint and David Weber

Available through Baen.com, booksellers, and used bookstores.

Also Available:

Grantville Gazette Volumes 1 – 102, magazine edited by Eric Flint, Paula Goodlett, Walt Boyes, Bjorn Hasseler. Available on 1632Magazine.com.

1632 Universe novels and "Eric Flint, Ring of Fire Series" on Baen.com

Recently Released and Forthcoming:

Ongoing: Baen has been re-releasing select 1632 books originally released by Eric Flint's Ring of Fire Press! Recent titles include three 1632 books by Bethanne Kim, one by Garrett W. Vance, one by Mike Watson, and two Time Spike novels by Garrett.

Forthcoming novels include re-releases of Ring of Fire Press works by Mark Huston, Kerryn Offord, and Karen and Kevin Evans. *1637: A Pilgrim's Passage* by Eric Flint and Griffin Barber will be released in August 2026. We hope you enjoy all the new releases!

Odd numbered months: New issues of Eric Flint's 1632 & Beyond

Reading Order:

There are three different reading orders available. The first is chronological. The second is by storyline. The third is by publication date. They can be found online at: https://author.1632magazine.com/canon-continuity/reading-order-small-bites/

Issue #17 May 2026

Eric Flint's 1632 & Beyond

Sarah Hayes
Iver Cooper
Garrett W. Vance
David Hankins
Bethanne Kim
Jack Carroll
John Deakins

ERIC FLINT'S 1632 & BEYOND ISSUE #17

This is a work of fiction. Names, characters places, and events portrayed in this book are fictional or used fictitiously. Any resemblance to real people (living or dead), events, or places is coincidental.

Editor-in-Chief Bjorn Hasseler
Production and Design Bethanne Kim
Editor Chuck Thompson
Cover Artwork by Cortney Skinner
Interior Art Garrett W. Vance

1. Science Fiction-Alternate History
2. Science Fiction-Time Travel

eBook ISBN: 978-1-962398-37-4
Paperback ISBN: 978-1-962398-38-1

Distributed by Flint's Shards Inc.
339 Heyward Street, #200
Columbia, SC 29201

Contents

Eric Flint's 1632 & Beyond

Bjorn Hasseler, Editor-in-Chief

Issue 17

Magdeburg Messenger (Fiction)

Issue 17's theme is Travel. It might be for business or pleasure, away from danger or toward it.

If you've read Sarah Hays' stories about Alyse Ballentine, you may remember an incident in Pomerania when Alyse went after stolen horses. "Ride For The Outfit" is that story. It takes place after "For Want Of A Nail" (Grantville Gazette 59), during "WWJD Is Not The Right Question" (Grantville Gazette 74), and earlier than "Before The Barbed Wire's Strung" (Grantville Gazette 91) and "One Woman's Treasure (Grantville Gazette 98).

"Have Rosary, Will Travel" is Iver P. Cooper's story about a professional pilgrim. Yes, that was a real job.

Garrett W. Vance's Japanese characters living in southeast Asia have been favorites since he first introduced them. Now, they are "At The Mouth Of The Mekong."

"The Breitenfeld Extraction" is David Hankins' third story. Dominick and Hildegard embark on a high-stakes rescue mission.

Alice Blower was a midwife in New England. In the new timeline, she journeys to Grantville.

The State Library Papers (1632 Non-Fiction)

Sometimes you want to communicate before you travel—or communicate instead of having to travel. Every book set in the Americas to date turns on communication or the lack thereof. Jack Carroll looks at the details of how some of this happens in "The North Atlantic Net."

When traveling, you should know what to expect. John Deakins explains why Native Americans might choose a different instrument of defense in "Bang Versus Twang In North America."

Patreon Supporters

1632 & Beyond thanks the following Patreon members who have generously agreed to help underwrite the magazine's operations.

Thank you so much for supporting us.

Gary

Pascal Durand

Marc Foppen

Sally Hardwick

Karjala Koponen

Jerry Johnson

MarcTyrrell

David Smith

Edh Stanley

Campbell Menzies

Thomas Williams

Virginia DeMarce

Jay Robison

Chuck Thompson

Magdeburg Messenger

Flint's Shards, Inc.

Ride For The Outfit

Sarah Hays

Somewhere In Pomerania

1637

"How's your Spanish?" Alyse asked, very quietly.

"In a textbook in Jena," the constable's wife responded. "I see you know whispers carry." Katherina Müllerin, midwife and trauma nurse, let her head fall back on the rock she'd been leaning against, a weary woman in a mistreated dress. "How about your German?"

"*Para este*," Alyse said, "*despacio y pequeño*." A hundred yards downstream, waters churned beneath the hooves of a patrol. Beyond, sun glittered back from helmets and pikes like sparklers off weapons. Effectively, their presence prevented Alyse and her three companions from crossing the stream on the way back to Grantville.

"Stay here," Alyse told her. "This goes like I hope, we'll get home in a few days."

"And if it doesn't?" The constable's wife had three years in Grantville to hone her command of up-time English; often, it made Alyse forget Katherina's down-time origin. In the past thirty-six hours they'd forged a practicing friendship out of the mess they'd fallen into together.

Alyse's blue-green eyes tightened as she bit her lip, then rolled sideways. Taking a twig, she sighted on where the sun should come through the clouds. "After dark tonight, y'all work back the way we came. Water'll be here." She drew a streak on the patch of bare ground. "Rest on the far side, drink what you can. Boil the water first." Handing over her match safe, crafted of interlocking shell casings, "Matches here, and"—a square of folded heavy foil appeared from her pocket—"You know how to make a cup without tearin' this?"

Katharina nodded.

"Moon's almost full tonight, so, once y'all are able, head this way." She drew an arrow away from the watercourse. "I'm not back by then, keep movin'. Make for Mecklenburg. Next little river's just about halfway."

Katharina grimaced.

"South of there, bear west. Don't look back, regardless." Before Katharina, watching the soldiers, could ask a question, Alyse vanished, her dirt-limned map scuffed out by a bootsole. The constable's wife sent a thoughtful look at the women the Texan had just left in her care as she sketched a cross in the air.

Halfway down the hill's backside, Alyse slid from rock to rock, staying in what cover she could find, toward a...did Germans call them *arroyos*? Dry wash, anyhow. She worked around the hill, downwind from the soldiers, wrinkling her nose. Lots of sweaty leather and hot metal among them, as well as horses nobody looked after properly.

Horses. It galled her to think how easily she might never again see the horses she'd left home to recover from a thief. "*Cuidado, muchacha*," Tio Matteo said in the back of her mind. "*No quieres perderlas*."

"*Pero los soldados, ahora, quiero mucho perderlos*," she argued under her breath, recalling something her mother had said. "*¿Viste cosas así en Vietnam*?"

"*Ah, si*." In her mind's eye, a summer evening after supper with the radio playing showed her a stocky man above middle height, silvery sparkles in his wavy black hair, corners of his mustache rising with the light in his soft brown eyes, his weathered South Texas vaquero's quick and dazzling smile. "*Pero eso fue la guerra*."

"Like this ain't." Cops-and-robbers on Air Force bases before the loss of her father, games of cowboys-and-Indians, despite being nearly too old for them, on a sprawl of ranchland after moving back to her mother's home, had come as close to war as she'd seen, before she married. Well, she'd learned things then. Hiding. Working from ambush. Saving ammunition, keeping quiet, finding cover as television cowboys had taught her. Memories kaleidoscoped, fading. "*Esto es, y nadie que me ayude*."

Grantville
A Week Earlier

"So," Claudette Green asked, once Alyce's estranged husband Powell left, "what would Adam Cartwright do?"

"What's right," Alyse answered. A knock on the door lifted her from her chair. "I better get started."

Her bootheels rang across the Mountain Top Baptist Bible Institute's kitchen but she barely heard the sound. She almost forgot her hat, left on the counter earlier as she helped an Institute lady bring in a bushel of tomatoes and squash, reveling in the scent of fresh vegetables; now, annoyed with herself for letting her husband upset her, she put the mouse-colored, sweat-marked Resistol on, trotting down the wooden steps a bare heartbeat ahead of a policeman coming in Claudette's office door. The Grantville police department had increased its original force by an order of magnitude since the Ring fell, but Alyse didn't want to tangle up today's necessities with a policeman's discussions. Especially not if, as experience insisted, that policeman spoke primarily some variation on early modern German.

Even the Castilian Spanish taught in Texas schools, with all its variations of preterit and case and person and gender, didn't have the curlicues and complications of early modern German, no two speakers of which she'd ever heard say the exact same thing in anything resembling the same way, she thought grumpily. "*Por que, Dios,*" she muttered, "did You drop Grantville into Germany and not Mexico, or even Spain, where at least I'd hear *una idioma bonita*?"

God, for whatever reason, didn't answer any more directly this time than the ten thousand or so others she'd asked. But in the back of her mind she heard her Uncle Matteo laughing softly. *"¡Un paso a la vez, sobrina! ¡No puedes ir màs ràpido sin caerte!"* Advice worth heeding. "Take a deep breath and calm down, Alyse."

The police Jeep Cherokee sat where Powell's Tahoe left a gap this pretty Saturday morning. Either the well-worn Cherokee or, more likely, the Tahoe had left a faint whiff of gasoline on the air; Alyse well knew Powell's habits with throttles. Honestly, that and the Suzuki 1100-cc he'd ridden had turned her head about him as much as his movie-star looks. The fast-moving bike's thrill had caught her heart more than his insurance agent's easy money and apparent interest in a community college rodeo rider.

Birdsong and the smell of new-cut hay interrupted her reminiscence. Still thinking about other things, Alyse bent her steps toward her mount. Claudette's invitation had seemed a good excuse to put some miles under the green-broke roan's saddle in Grantville's mix of traffic: pedestrians, wagons, autos, teams, riders, donkey carts, bicycles, and now and then a wheelbarrow.

This morning she'd been pleased when the roan took the three-wheel, steam-powered "ATV" they'd encountered at the bottom of the Mountain Top drive in stride. Well, she'd been distracted when its driver, or rider, turned out to be Orlando Rosales de Circassia under a helmet and goggles. She hadn't seen him in months.

"Lando!"

"Alyse!" He laughed, stepping off to clasp her hand. "Look at this train of mules, would you?"

"Fifty-eight head, I make it, and ore wagons," she agreed. "Where do you reckon they're going?"

He shrugged. "Just cutting through the Ring of Fire on their way from up around Erfurt to the new Redbird Institute. How are you?"

"*Muy bien, gracias, amigo*. How are you?" Alyse said.

"Very well, and my darling wife is even better. You know, the only good thing about this"—his gesture took in his three-wheeled vehicle, its long nose adorned with a small steam engine, its wide posterior bins piled with a mix of small packages and smaller firewood—"is that I'm home every night. Much as I miss my good white mule, so many miles in a day we could not cover together." He shook his head in wonder. "H.A. Burston makes life interesting."

"I hear you," she said. "But he's been pretty easy for us to work for, so far."

"You," he said, "are lucky, then. Well, that's the last ore wagon. See you soon, I hope!" He scampered back into his...saddle? pilot's chair?...where, with a kick of one lever and a twist of another, he made his way south to Grantville on Route 250.

A quarter-hour later, she'd entered Claudette's front parlor, where the pastor's wife conducted the business of talking to members of her congregation on personal matters. In the quiet way good friends sometimes do, Claudette Greene had ambushed Alyse, whose intention had been to have a pleasant visit with her pastor's wife, pay upcoming daycare and pre-school fees, and put in a little light fresh-air exercise. For the last few weeks she'd been stuck at home between physical therapy appointments; that had cut her expenses for childcare dramatically. Cleared for work, she wanted those arrangements made—and paid for. Especially now that she'd need the youngest to stay extra nights while she went after her company's stolen horses, she wanted those arrangements settled. The ones with her partner would be tough enough.

Alyse could still taste the adrenaline burn in the back of her throat. The visit had not gone the way Claudette intended. In nigh six years since the Ring fell, important jobs took Powell elsewhere, first with the Army, then the government, for more than four and a half of those years. The harder Alyse tried to show Powell the fruits of her labor and the advantages of keeping their paid-for home, the more he chafed at her resistance.

Her letters, pleading and proud, grew shorter; his, demanding and curt, stopped mentioning their tidy house, then the children, then their marriage. Alyse doubted, now, that anything she did could mend that breach. Worse, she didn't feel angry or sad, but mostly just tired about the whole situation. Today, her own mood created an air about her that kept other people from crossing her path. She adjusted her hat, not quite noticing how people stepped out of her way as she pulled the horse's reins from around a hitch rail.

The roan snuffled; Alyse pulled a dried apple slice from a pocket and offered it to the young horse. Positive reinforcement made itself second nature dealing with horses, just as with two-legged students. A quick check of her cinches preceded a boot into a stirrup and a swing into her saddle; lifting her reins, she touched heels to the roan, who pulled up and tossed a startled head at the sight—or maybe scent, with that gasoline tang still in the air—of the parked Cherokee. Alyse let the horse spend a minute looking, listening, and sniffing before urging her mount closer. They had time, this early afternoon, for one more unusual thing to go from being scary to ordinary in the horse's mind, Alyse figured. After the horse calmed down, she headed into town; if Powell had gone to the house, she didn't want to meet him there. She needed to talk to her partner anyway.

* * *

"*Hola*," Pedro Sebastian de Treviño greeted her, from the rocker on the office's porch. When the weather allowed, he preferred doing the company books there. "*¿Como estas hoy?¿Qué te trae aquí ahora*?"

She'd been supposed to have today off. "*Muy bien, gracias*," she answered. "Seen Luis?"

Pedro Sebastian's quick grin vanished in sober consideration. "Yes. He stopped by to tell me that we had almost all our working horses stolen. He says he saw Gerhard Rutger taking them, but could not stop him. He called the police, but all they could do was take a report."

Alyse nodded. "I couldn't stop Gerhard either. We called the police. They don't have enough manpower to send anybody looking. They said they'd telegraph Bamberg and let the marshals and Mounted Constabulary know."

"This is not a surprise," he said gravely. "We need our horses back, lest our business fail."

Alyce's blue-green eyes iced over. "You know that. I know that. Luis knows that. My kids know that. Powell knows it too, but he says it's the cops' job, and if they can't do it, too bad." Her disgust colored her voice. "I think I told you I'm cleared to come back to work, if I stay off green horses—and out of fights."

He gave her a rueful smile. "Out of fights is easier than off green horses. Between the remounts we need and getting horses ready for students, that's half our business these days."

Alyse nodded. "I know."

He walked her into the office and pulled out a chair. "I know you broke your collarbone. How close is it, really, to healing?"

"I rode that fresh-broke roan up to Mountain Top this morning," she answered. "Didn't have any static. Even saw Lando Rosales on that steam-powered three-wheeler H.A. Burston's replacing his mule with."

"Our investor," Pedro Sebastian said, "is not a man lacking whimsy."

"*Es cierto*," she replied judiciously; he laughed softly.

"I imagine we will find out how much of a fight we must win if we stay in business," Pedro Sebastian said. "A visitor from the Grantville Police asked me to sign a complaint. He advises that if we want our horses back, we must find them and bring them ourselves. It will shut us down a couple weeks, at least—maybe a month, to attend to that. I do not like to think of what effect that might have."

"That's what I came to talk to you about." The Texan looked up at him, aslant, intent. "I don't think we, as in you and me, should do any such thing. You, as in *el jefe del negocio*, should stay put. Keep the doors open, books balanced, bills paid, customers happy on the courier side, and students busy on the school side. Also, look after your family."

"And what do you think you should do?" he asked mildly. He thought he knew her answer before he heard it. Her words just confirmed what he expected.

"Get our livestock back, and that horse-thief into jail, if I can."

The look he gave her came with a long, low whistle. "If you can?"

"Last time I had anything like this to do, I hadn't turned twenty-six years old yet."

Pomerania

Present Day

She felt like a kid again, bellied-down in the best cover she could find, watching her opposition move along, breathing quietly so as not to give away her position. Although she ached more, tired faster, needed to think instead of react, she'd slipped right back into those pre-teen cowboys-and-outlaws reflexes, except for the lack of any sort of weapon.

Of course, she hadn't been able to talk Paul Santee into even the loan of a single modern firearm. Nor had all those lessons with Sally McQuade's dad done anything toward making her a "fast gun." Just an accurate one, more so with her right hand than her left. She decided next time she saw Santee she'd find out if he had any converted Colt percussion handguns he might part with, now that every single thing he could scrounge up didn't have to stay forever in Grantville's emergency arsenal; maybe a Patterson or Dragoon, though she doubted she could stand up to the recoil of a Walker. Five rounds to the cylinder would've still been better than...nothing. Not even throwable rocks had come handy.

Four days out on Rutger's trail she'd come across the holed-up gang, stolen horses and all, a few miles out of Stettin. Four men with Gerhard Rutger. Only she found them playing with stolen goods other than her horses. She watched, increasingly sick to her stomach, while the bunch took turns pushing the women—well, two women and a girl—around.

Here or there a rough grab turned to a forced kiss; when the youngest one objected to an even rougher embrace, the horse thief's slap sounded like a gunshot as the wiry brunette went sprawling.

Alyse never thought about what to do next. With a hop into the saddle, she set spurs to her tough little bay, slid the seven-and-a-half-inch Solingen Bowie out of her *chaparejos'* built-in sheath, and rode down into the camp with a long-drawn-out Texas yell.

It didn't go like the movies, or the old after-school TV westerns.

A couple flintlocks went off. She heard the buzz of a lead ball, but by that time she'd kicked Rutger in the head with a *tapadero* stirrup-and-boot and run the horse right over one of the other men. She spurred another down the ribs. The women broke for the woods once they understood whose side Alyse rode in on.

A blow like a baseball bat whacked her out of her saddle, and the bay kept running. Alyse landed on her feet, swapping ends with the knife to throw it with all her strength. It hit hilt-first, but the man it struck between the eyes went down. Alyse twisted out of a grasp, threw her elbow backward as she went, and bent at the knees, pitching somebody into the dirt. Free of his hold, she kicked him upside the head for good measure. She shouted and slapped the stolen horses into a run. A different flintlock sounded. Knowing she'd done everything she could, she dove behind a tree, pulled herself to her feet, and ran the way the women had gone.

Thirty hours later, Alyse parked the three women as safely as she could and started sliding down the back of the ridge. Most of two days on foot with nothing but her own pockets' contents, the women trying to be brave in spite of being lost, tired, hungry, and sure they'd fallen into hands at least as savage as their kidnappers', had worn Alyse's patience entirely away.

Not to mention being bone-weary, absolutely filthy, and half-starved; or that she'd last tasted coffee the morning before she'd ridden down on Rutger's bunch with more fury than forethought. She decided, now, to try to find whatever she might to fight with. Here, for example: a length of some kind of very sturdy vine.

"*Gracias a Dios*," she murmured, remembering that poison ivy and oak didn't grow in Europe. Thorns did, though, reminding her of the *brasada* at home.

By the time she got back to the water's edge, the soldiers had moved on. She curled the vine into a coil, studied the tracks on the riverbank, considered what she saw...and picked up a knife somebody had dropped. Or thrown away: it had a broken handle and a blade nearly dull as a hoe. Alyse found empty wine bottles in the patrol's debris field, too, from the cold meal made while its horses rested and drank.

She lifted her head, listening hard; a breeze brushed her bangs toward her eyes. The soldiers hadn't left anything else worthwhile behind, and in disgust she kicked extra dirt over noisome things they had. Then she returned to Katharina and the others, still careful but not so slow this time.

"They're gone. Makin' for Mecklenburg, so we prob'ly shouldn't."

"Agreed."

"Nothin' for it now until they're far enough away." Alyse dropped cross-legged to the ground. She handed over the bottles, adorned with pebbles for corks and slings made from part of the vine. "'Least we'll have a way to carry water."

She didn't say anything about the knife; it lived, now, tucked behind the edge of her chaps. She closed her eyes. Nobody spoke; in a few minutes the sounds of the woods—breeze and birds and small critters going about their daily business—took over; she settled her back against a tree, intending to keep watch while the women rested until the water cleared up from the soldiers' crossing.

Alyse came awake all at once. Katharina and the women with her—a girl Alyse figured for seventeen or so called Anna, a woman of twenty-five or -six called Margueretha, both some sort of kin of the constable's wife, neither yet sure their nightmare of a kidnapping had ended—stared at her in horror. Not six feet away stood a boar, snuffling, chomping.

It took a half second to get her feet under her, a full second more to find a fist-sized rock and throw it, hard. The rock hit an eye. The animal straightened up, turning away. Alyse picked up another, flung it as hard, hit between ear and eye. The boar turned further. When a third rock struck, it ran.

Daylight had dwindled to evening while she slept. Alyse turned to Katharina. "We should go."

The water in the river reached mid-thigh on Alyse, chaps slung over a shoulder to keep them dry, watching her footing as she went. Once across, she spoke just loud enough for Katharina to hear. "It's slick, but there's no real deep holes. Tie your shoes together. Tuck your skirts up to stay dry. Water's cold."

Katharina nodded, shoved her shoes through the jug-handle knot she'd tied around her water bottle, then motioned the others to follow. They crossed one after the other, and on the far bank Alyse, noting their shivers and blue lips, quietly put together a fire no bigger than the brim of her hat. Katharina and her charges watched. Alyse filled the former wine bottles from the river, brought the water to a boil and poured it out, carefully, making sure to clean the tops of the bottles and the pebbles in the flow, filled and boiled them again. All four had gone at least two days with neither food nor water; once the second batch boiled, Alyse poured enough in the foil cup to pass around.

Margueretha cupped hands around the foil, holding still for a long ten-count before sipping and passing the vessel to Anna, who imitated her.

Alyse tipped another bottle, swallowing without touching her mouth, then passed it to Katharina.

"There are," Katharina said, "greens, if we had a way to cook them." Margueretha ripped some pieces from the already-ragged end of a petticoat and braided them, leaving a pouch no bigger than her thumb in the middle. She spoke earnestly to Katharina, who nodded and told Alyse, "She used to look after sheep for her father. She says she thinks she can get some meat."

"Supper," Alyse said, and pulled herself to her feet. "Sounds like a plan. Are y'all dry yet?"

"*Nein*," Anna said. "*Mir ist kalt und nass. Das ist deine Schuld.*"

The words might not have sunk in but the meaning did.

"*Lo siento*," Alyse had to be polite with these women, but she didn't have to swallow all her irritation; she took it out in language. "*Pero todos vivos, hasta ahora*."

The distinctive "thock" of a rock hitting something sounded again; soon Margueretha reappeared, a brace of pigeon-size birds dangling from each hand. Alyse went digging among cattails. Anna helped Katharina gather greens. The prospect of a hot meal preoccupied them all. The fire burned down; rolling the whole birds in wet mud, Alyse settled them on some coals and heaped more over them. Anna donated a camisole scrap to wrap the greens for steaming atop cattail tubers on a green-wood grate.

Once the bottles of water boiled again, Alyse said to Katharina, "Keep an eye on stuff."

"*Was machst du?*" Margeuretha asked. Despite the doubtful eye she'd cast on Alyse's methods, she could smell roast fowl now too.

"*Platos*," Alyse said, "*y tapas*." In high school she'd been taught that straight translation from Spanish to German couldn't be done. At least the early modern era helped prove that contention wrong, she thought. The memory lifted a corner of her mouth in what would, if it grew up, be a smile.

Her dull salvaged knife made cutting bark from a deadfall harder than it needed to be, but by the time she'd fashioned two trenchers and a cup, even Anna understood enough to want to help. Alyse handed her a slice of bark and showed her the cup, and the youngster began to fashion a second vessel.

"About that knife," Katharina said. "I saw Rutger take yours."

"I aim to have mine back," Alyse answered. "But somebody didn't want this, and we can use it." Deftly, she cleaned forked branches. "Spoons'd be better, but this'll get us by now."

With a branch she unburied the birds, cracking the baked-mud shells with the knife's haft. Feathers came off in the mud; Alyse divided the birds into halves. Margueretha, joining in the spirit of a hot meal, poured the greens' broth into bark cups, chopping greens into bite-size pieces. The soup, or tea, tasted vaguely of sage and thyme. Alyse enjoyed all of it she drank.

She refilled the water bottles then settled down by the fire, rock in one hand and knife in the other. With a broader stick, Katharina made a pit by the fire where she buried the birds' well-gnawed bones, entrails, and feather-studded mud shells. Alyse lifted a brow at her as she raked ashes over and into the dirt.

"To keep away wild things," the constable's wife said. "We should set a watch, no?"

"I c'n sit up a while. Y'all get some sleep. I'll wake you when I'm tired enough."

"Two on, two off. Anna with you." Katharina, who'd clearly heard enough of her husband's reports on field operations to internalize basic lessons, directed the younger woman to do that. Alyse found herself impressed with the younger girl when she asked, "*Wie viele Stunden*?"

Katharina looked at Alyse, who shrugged.

"*Drei*," Katharina said.

Anna nodded. "*Möchten Sie, dass wir wie Wachen am Rand des Lagers entlanggehen?*"

Katharina saw the look on Alyse's face. "She's gone hunting with her father and brothers. She wants to know if you want to walk the camp like sentries?"

"That ain't a bad idea," Alyse said. "She'd have to step real quiet and carry a big stick."

Katharina reported that to Anna, who nodded. Alyse returned to her deadfall and broke off a limb barely thicker than her wrist, the length of her arm. She looked at Anna then swung the limb like a baseball bat. The girl gave a nod.

Midnight came and went; the moon set. Alyse nudged Katharina awake. "You be okay 'til daylight?"

Katharina took the cup Alyse offered. "Sure. Let me wake Margueretha."

"Daylight," Alyse said. "Don't wait ‘til sunup. Need to move soon as we can."

"I understand," Katharina said. "How's Anna?"

"Walked about a half dozen miles," Alyse said. "She's gonna do to ride the river with, I reckon."

Katharina looked puzzled. Margueretha finished a cup of soup, took Anna's stick and began walking. Back-to-back, five steps from the fire Katharina had rekindled, Alyse and Anna lay down. Alyse slept almost before she landed, elbow under cheekbone.

Katharina woke them as lemon light outlined the horizon. Not a lot of cloud, Alyse noticed, with a stiff breeze bustling out of the north. Anna sat up. Margeuretha handed them bark vessels of tea—warm, this time. Gratefully, Alyse drank. Not coffee, she thought, but still, *mejor que nada*.

It took them all day, following water, to find a settlement. The soldiers' trail had faded, or turned off, before they found the town. Alyse bartered her silky blue bandanna for bread and a wooden spoon. Anna and Margueretha talked their way into jobs waiting tables and washing mugs in the tavern, and Alyse earned them all a night in a hayloft by cleaning stalls.

When daylight came again, they had slept and eaten; Alyse felt better. Her companions looked and sounded like they'd had their first real break in weeks. One of Margueretha's coins went for an egg-size lump of soap and a two-pint metal bowl, much-mended; one of Anna's for a wooden comb. Alyse swapped all her shirt's spare buttons of shiny plastic for a muslin sack. That night, and the next, the women camped within sound of water, though not the same stream.

A roll of braided horsehair and a scrap of leather had come into Anna's possession; the second night, she crafted a sturdy bow and sharpened-stick arrows. Now everybody had some sort of weapon: Margueretha her sling, Anna her bow, Katharina her big stick, and Alyse her knife. Perhaps they didn't, the Texan thought, quite add up to a wrecking crew, but they all walked easier on the trail. She'd taken up using a flint spall and the back of the knife to spark their fires, saving matches. Between the bow and the sling, they ate better, too.

The third morning, they crossed a trail Alyse had seen before: Rutger's outfit, and the stolen horses—the tracks and sign hadn't been here more than a few hours. Her companions seemed reluctant to follow; Alyse explained the whole reason she'd left Grantville: get these horses back, take this thief to justice. Katharina had reasons for wanting to see the gang who'd taken them hostage not run loose any more, and Margueretha, too, had a spark in her eye contemplating how to bring down the men who had treated them so miserably.

Only Anna still seemed scared.

"You," Alyse had Katharina explain, "can stay hidden and shoot arrows at them." The girl didn't look reassured. The older women talked to her for what felt like half an hour, but she stayed mule-headed about following the tracks.

"Or you can hide and watch," Alyse said. "Somebody'll need to take word back if this goes sideways." That, she noted, didn't just get through but jarred the youngster's worldview, evidently.

The young woman asked a hesitant question. "*Du würdest mir zutrauen, das alleine zu machen*?"

"Pretty much got to," Alyse told Katharina. "Five of them, three of us. Leaves Anna. What she does is her choice, I reckon." She picked up one of Anna's arrows, split the point with her knife and stuck in a spall of flint off her cobble. With a couple strands of hair, Alyse bound the stem back, hard enough to hold the point.

" *Was is das*?"

"Piece of sharp rock, horsehair string, and a bit of feather, first thing you know you can't tell it from somethin' the souvenir shop sells—and claims a Comanche built." She picked up a wingfeather from one of Margueretha's breakfast prizes. "These things are good for more'n making quill pens, too."

It took a minute to split the quill into three pieces and bind them with another strand of hair. Then she motioned for the bow, nocked the arrow, and took aim at a tree a hundred yards away. Almost no sound accompanied the shot, but the shaft drove past the rock into the bark.

Anna stared at her. " *Woher weißt du das*?"

"I grew up without money," Alyse answered when Katharina translated. "But I had a library card and a whole ranch to pick stuff up off of, so if

I could read about it I'd build it. I tried a lot of stuff—bows, slingshots, about anything I could hunt with. Fishing gear, too."

"But you didn't build a slingshot," Katharina said, cutting Margueretha off.

"No rubber bands. Slingshots I know how to build need somethin' stretchy to make 'em work. With a bow, you just need springy wood and a stout string." Pensively, she added, "And time to flake the points."

Katharina shook her head. "But...you'd been taught to use a gun."

"Didn't mean I could afford one, let alone ammunition," Alyse said. Seventh-grade Texas history classes went marching through her memory. "It hadn't been a hundred fifty years, yet, when I was growin' up, since the Plains Indians were the finest light cavalry on Earth. A bow's a fast repeater. Take yea-many arrows"—she put her hands together in a circle—"and you c'n outshoot most firearms white folks used, before the Texas Revolution. Good part of what most of 'em had through the War Between the States."

"Which compares how, with what we might be chasing right now?" Katharina asked.

"*En realidad, bastante bien*," Alyse said. "Um, actually quite good. Far as I know none of those hoodlums has any kind of up-time weaponry, or even any of the new stuff from Suhl. Comin' in to get you loose, I saw flintlocks and some almighty big knives, but not anything I'd call a rifle."

"Arquebuses and short swords," Katharina said. Alyse looked at her, inquiringly. "Well. Or muskets. Depends who they stole from."

A grin threatened to do more than shift the shape of Alyse's gaze, lightening her expression. "Same as it ever was," she said quietly. "*Perezosos que no sirven nada*."

Katharina turned, explaining in rapid-fire early modern German. Presently Margueretha tapped Alyse's forearm. "*Kannst du mehr machen?*"

"Maybe." Alyse looked around: Woods-decorated soil beneath their feet consisted mostly of loam, with not much rock. "Keep your eyes open; we might find makings as we go."

Margueretha nodded firmly. Then she marched over and pulled the arrow out of the tree. It came away with the rock still in place, and she looked mildly impressed.

"*Zu Hause machen die Jäger diese mit Metallspitzen,*" Anna said.

Margueretha didn't hand her the arrow, examining it as they walked on. "*Siehst du hier Schmieden oder Minen, Mädchen? Denk nach. Alte Gewohnheiten sind keine schlechten Gewohnheiten.*"

Anna looked mildly abashed, but said nothing.

Alyse picked up the odd acorn or similar pebble, passing them to Margueretha. "Don't waste good material."

Katharina laughed. "You're telling her what she told Anna."

"Tell 'em I said they'll do to ride the river with," Alyse answered. "I figure you know you will too."

The older woman gave her a long look. "And how do you know that?"

"You're still here." She spent a minute looking along the tracks they followed, listening carefully. The woods sounded like nothing bothered the birds or critters. "We're a while behind 'em. Need it not to rain, or we'll lose the trail."

"Won't we anyway, since they're ahead and we're afoot?"

A shrug. "Depends where they're headed and whether they stop."

"And if we stop?"

"We'll have to, but we can always pick up their trail again." She put one foot in front of the other. Where the trail followed a defile, Alyse led over the hill's shoulder—and cut down the riders' lead visibly. When they crossed it again, the sign looked, and smelled, considerably fresher. "*¿Podrías mirar eso?*"

Spread out on a pocket-sized meadow between the hills grazed the horses, except those Rutger and companions sat astride in a relaxed fashion.

Katharina said, "What are they doing?"

"Looks like waitin' for somethin'," Alyse said. "Or maybe somebody."

"Hold up," Katharina said suddenly, putting a hand on Alyse's forearm. "Hear that?" Traffic: thump of hoofs, creak of leather, jingle of bits.

"Get the girls under cover, and you too," Alyse said. She flattened, shading her eyes to watch; three riders approached Rutger's gang. One of his companions waved a greeting. Curt commands followed, but Rutger's nearest companion objected loudly. In another minute the situation devolved: a saber slammed flat across the objector's temple, knocking him from his saddle.

Rutger pulled a pistol from his belt and sent a choking wad of smoke into the air. The man who'd knocked Rutger's partner off his mount rode straight into the horse thief. Alyse flinched as her bay went to her knees, but she rolled over and came back to her feet.

Meanwhile Rutger lay in the dirt, still enough he might be dead.

Another rider pushed between him and the stolen horses, careless whether or not Rutger's dismounted partner went under the hoofs of what looked like a well-trained warhorse. Alyse bit her lip, watching. The three riders made short work of Rutger's partners despite more billows of bitter powder-smoke rising through the air. In less than two minutes, they had knocked all five senseless; three minutes more and they'd rifled pockets. One snagged a money-belt, and all the thieves' firearms went into the newcomers' belts or sashes, charges spent or not. Not long afterward they departed, one spitting on Rutger as they turned to ride away.

"*Madre de Dios y todos los santos*," Alyse murmured. "*No hay honor entre ladrones.*"

"Why didn't they take the horses?" Katharina wanted to know.

"They got what they wanted—guns, money, stuff that's easy to carry, hard to trace, fast to sell," Alyse answered over her shoulder. "Thought I told you to take cover."

"Cover doesn't mean I have to be blind," Katharina said. "Just hidden."

"That's a fact," the Texan allowed. "Come on, we've got to get down there. If we can get them tied up and on horses, we've got half a day's light to start home."

"What if the others come back?"

She chuckled darkly. "*Entonces tendremos que averiguar qué sigue*."

Alyse slipped and slid down the hill, and began talking softly as soon as she hit level ground. The bay filly lifted her head, turned to look, then walked up to Alyse, nudging her hard. Alyse ran a hand over every leg, producing dry apple slices from a pocket to offer the willing horse. While the filly chewed, she looked around.

There, on a roan with its head hanging down, sat a packsaddle; Alyse's good grass rope had bound on a heavy sack, before the thieves had cut it loose to take.

Anna arrived next. She watched a moment, then began to help Alyse bind their prey. When four had been thoroughly trussed and the fifth pronounced deceased from the warhorse's hoof caving in his head, Katharina and Margueretha began looking through the scattered belongings strewn about, hunting for their own. Alyse hadn't bothered; she had to figure out how to get the senseless men over packhorses.

"They stink," Katharina observed.

"They do," Alyse assented. "Not all of them're dead yet though."

"Smell better if they were," the constable's wife offered.

"Could be," Alyse said.

She didn't wish out loud for single-trees or pulleys. It wouldn't help. But a twenty-foot length of rope remained whole, and a thigh-thick low limb offered possibilities. She flung the rope's end over.

"You're not going to hang them," Katharina said firmly. An avowed Jimmy Stewart fan, she had spent last night's can't-fall-asleep time explaining *The Ox-Bow Incident* to Alyse, who hadn't seen it.

"No," Alyse said. "Well, not like that. But do you want us trying to put one of these *pendejos* over a horse while the others wake up?"

Katharina thought about that. "Could we?" She looked doubtfully over the men, of whom Gerhard Rutger looked the smallest. "He's got to weigh two hundred pounds.""More," Alyse said mildly. Her fingers had kept working; now a bowline hung just above the height of her eyes. The free end brushed the ground at her feet. She threaded that through the rope around Rutger's wrists, then through the bowline, and snugged the result against the limb. She picked up the longest remaining fragment of rope and dallied it around the bay filly's saddlehorn, noting with pleasure that while the horse had been working, she hadn't been mistreated.

"Few more minutes, *mi hija*," she said. In her saddlebags, which apparently nobody had plundered yet, she had more dried apples. With a hand on the bay's mane and another on the horn, Alyse swung into her saddle. It felt good to be back where she belonged: in Texas-crafted leather on the back of a horse, pulling a rope's load like taking another maverick to a branding fire. She guided the bay back until Rutger's body nearly stood erect. "Whoa, girl. Hold him here."

A few seconds and she had the packsaddled roan under the weight. "Give me a hand, ladies?"

Katharina grinned, said something quick and sharp, and the others moved to her side.

"Put his feet over the far side," Alyse said. She felt the weight change and grabbed the rope lashing Rutger's boots together. "That'll do."

Another minute, another hunk of rope, and she had knotted the lashings holding his wrists and the ones that held his legs together.

"The same with the others?" Katharina asked.

"It won't be as easy without packsaddles," Alyse started to warn, but Margueretha spoke low and fast and Anna laughed out loud.

"Like chickens for market, she says," Katharina supplied.

Alyse watched them handle ropes and weights with the ease of a lifetime's practice; farm life taught women that. While Anna ran the loose end of the rope from the limb through first one, then another, then the last of the thieves' bindings, Alyse used her old entrenching tool in a claybank, rolled in the dead man and piled the spoil over him. When the women finished, all four men had been tied belly-down and snug over hackamored packhorses.

"It's like tying poultry to carry, only bigger," Katharina explained as the last knots creaked into place. "I do think..." Her voice trailed off. "The trip home will feel better.'

Alyse nodded firmly. "Go faster, too, horseback."

Anna spoke, then Margueretha; it didn't sound as much like an argument as a question-and-answer. Katharina looked interested at Margueretha's query, then surprised. "Will it make up the time you spent burying that one?"

"No doubt," the Texan answered. "D'y'all know how?"

"You...show. We do." Anna spoke.

"Get started, then." Alyse gathered up the saddled horses. She looked dubiously at the ankle-length skirts her companions wore, then shrugged. Slowly, she sorted the mounts: the sorrel she'd worked with the most, an older blue roan she knew for a farmhorse, and a leggy Arab-faced gray.

"I've ridden before," Katharina said.

Alyse gave her the gray's reins. "You know how to deal with saddle sores?"

The constable's wife nodded tightly. "Done some of that too."

"We'll do some more," Alyse led Margueretha to the roan. "Ever done this before?"

The woman shook her head.

"Relax," Alyse told her. She breathed in, then out, both deeply, and scratched the roan's withers reassuringly before she checked the girths. The horse blew out a breath; Alyse snugged the cinches before the wily animal could puff out again. "That ought to hold you."

Margueretha looked apprehensive, but not terrified; Alyse told Katharina, "She'll need to put her left foot in the stirrup, and swing her right leg over. Put that foot in the other stirrup and let me adjust the length—she's not as tall as Rutger."

"None of us is," Katharina answered smartly. Alyse chuckled, bending knee against leather. "Step here." She held both hands against her thigh, reins over the saddlehorn. Katharina explained; Margueretha hesitantly set her foot in Alyse's hands. She shifted weight, the Texan gave a lift, and suddenly Margueretha sat in the saddle, looking pleased and scared all at once.

A low laugh escaped the Texan. *"Eso no estuvo tan mal."* She adjusted the stirrup leathers and slid Margueretha's much-worn shoes into the stirrups. "Put your weight here, when the horse's moving."

Margueretha leaned in. Alyse made a mental note not to ever let a horse run with her. Anna had been watching eagerly. Now she walked up to the sorrel, rubbed its withers as she had seen Alyse do, and grabbed the saddle horn and the horse's mane. She gave a little jump and swung aboard, a rein in each hand like plowlines.

"Farm kid," Alyse muttered. But she hadn't started out any better; nor had Anna had the benefit of Tio Matteo and a whole family of *Kenedeños* to teach her. Katharina mounted the gray; Alyse handed her a lead-line for two of the packhorses. She walked past Anna, checking rigging for all her charges. Four packhorses, four ridden, four on lead-ropes. All Rutger's thievery recovered, including the tack and gear just as they'd been when Rutger and his accomplices stole the horses. Alyse checked the saddlebags, but the mesquite-handled Bowie she'd lost getting the women out of the gang's clutches didn't turn up.

None of the horses looked much worse for wear, though they hadn't had decent care or currying. She could fix that once she got them safe, Alyse decided. Halfway between sundown and dark she found a comfortable stopping place. They'd covered a good few miles, not making the horses do more than a steady walk. Here, they could water the horses, let them graze, and have a wind break.

She thought about taking the thieves off the packhorses, but nothing nearby would be as handy for getting them back on as had the limb she'd used to hoist them into place. One growled something as she passed, but the others either hadn't come to yet or didn't care to make a noise.

"He says he needs a latrine," Katharina supplied.

"Tell him we don't have one," Alyse answered. Words passed between the two; Katharina bopped the complainant smartly across the back of his head with her stick, turning him slack as a sack of potatoes.

Alyse decided not to interfere.

She took Anna with her for the first watch, supper having been pulled out of various saddlebags. The girl moved stiffly, but not badly. The horses munched, not straining the hobbles Alyse had contrived. The women had water and a bright but not-too-big fire.

"Come daylight," Alyse told Anna, "You're going to be sore."

"You...will not?"

"Not as much," the Texan answered. "Comes from spendin' a lot of time in a saddle."

The girl walked up, deliberately touching Alyse's face, then ran a thumb under her jaw. The fingers tightened subtly while the thumb explored her throat. "*Was bist du? kein Mann? keine Frau?*"

Adam's apple, Alyse thought. Or is she tryin' to find whiskers? Well, I ain't fixin' to show her under my shirt. Fighting back a slap to keep the girl from choking her, she let a smile rise to her eyes. "*Soy Tejana*," she said. "*No hombre. Mujer.*"

"*Nein, nicht dass ich wüsste.*" The brunette looked stubborn and confu sed. "*Du klingst wie eine Frau. Du benimmst dich wie ein Mann. Was bist du?*"

Fair enough, Alyse thought; she savvied the German's gist, if it went by slow enough. Lots of folks here and now had never heard of Texas, never mind Rangers, let alone Cordell Walker; she herself hadn't found out about Wade Harper, or his great-grandpa Jess until just before the Ring fell. "Grew up a tomboy, even for a Texan."

Anna's hand dropped and she moved away.

"Katharina," Alyse said in a low voice, back at the fire. The constable's wife, weary, expecting heaven knew what kind of trouble now, looked up. "What?"

"How do I tell this kid I'm what I have to be?"

"That kid," Katharina said, "has to do the same. You want me to explain?"

"I'd rather speak for myself, this time, but I need to know she'll understand."

Katharina sighed. "Then here's what you say, and try to keep that Texas drawl out of it. '*Ich bin, was ich sein muss. Du machst das Gleiche, nicht wahr?*'"

Alyse ran over the words in her mind, then repeated them out loud. Katharina flapped a hand. "That drawl," she muttered. "But it comes through in everything, so just go on."

With a cup of coffee from the pot beside the fire in hand, Alyse walked back. She repeated the words Katharina had suggested, and then held out the cup.

Anna pushed the drink away. *"Nein, danke."*

Alyse shrugged, pulled half the cup down in a long swallow, and grinned faintly. She had missed coffee, and she meant to catch up every chance she got.

Morning brought complaints from all the prisoners about needing a latrine. Alyse considered her pack horses' skins and got the women to help her take their captives down, one at a time, for a trip to a shallow pit in the woods. Once all of them had had a turn, she picked out a water bottle and brought it over for each to have a drink. She marked that bottle with a fragment of rag through the handle-loop, then marched each captive to a smaller rock.

"Step up," she said. Katharina repeated the order, brandishing her stick, as Alyse led a packhorse— different from yesterday's—close enough to kick the back of a knee out from under a trussed thief. That dropped him hard enough over the horse to knock the breath out of him. She bound the ropes as before, following suit with the rest. The riders left the place as they'd found it except for buried ashes and a filled-in field latrine.

Alyce avoided towns. She was sure they'd left Pomerania. This could be Brandenburg or it could be Mecklenburg, and she didn't know whom she could trust.

Late in the afternoon of the fourth day they came upon a town on the outskirts of Magdeburg. Rutger and his gang could be held in the *rathaus'* basement jail overnight. Alyse quietly had Katharina advise the jailer not to leave them without a guard; when he asked why, she gave him her name with some tense instructions in a language Alyse barely recognized. The jailer gave a shout, and a boy appeared. Terse commands followed.

The youngster fled; a couple hours later he returned with two men who looked a cross between unbelieving and anxious. One of them, a substantial fellow much taller than usual, went first to Margueretha's side, then Katharina's. Tears began to trickle down Margueretha's face as he wrapped her in his arms. It took a while, but Alyse learned that the tall fellow was their brother; the second newcomer turned out to be Anna's father, who'd been searching for the missing women several days, riding widening circles out from the farmstead the thieves had used while they waited for Rutger.

Upon discovering the women's disappearance, these men had dispatched Katharina's twelve-year-old son straight for Sangerhausen, to rouse the constable. Several minutes passed while all this knowledge percolated through the weary women. Three received family members' embraces; Alyse stood a little aside, every line of her body utterly weary.

"A courier will go to Grantville," Katharina said, "if you wish. We all have rooms arranged for tonight here. Supper and baths are waiting."

"Obliged," Alyse said. "I've got to get my horses taken care of first, though."

Anna's father, graying and lean but fit and nimble, said something Katharina explained as, "Of course. Willem wants to know how he can help."

She fished the last coin out of the pocket inside her vest. "Help me find a stable?"

A gesture, quick words between father and daughter, then Willem stepped up to push Alyse's coin back toward her pocket. "*Meine Tochter ist dank Ihnen sicher zu Hause. Ich kümmere mich um die Kosten. Was brauchen Sie?"*

In early modern Germany a livery complete with water, hay, and stalls would likely exist, Alyse thought, by some name she might not recognize; but if she wanted good hay, clean water, and maybe a hand with her recovered horses' care, it wouldn't do to ask shyly any more than to seem too broke to pay. "Twelve horses, tell him; good hay, grain, clean water, and a proper brushing."

* * *

The constable arrived halfway through the night, pounding on the door of the inn where the town had put the women up as though he meant to break it down himself. Head and shoulders taller than any of the women, he still wore trail-used clothes. Katharina's gray-streaked auburn bun fit neatly under his chin. He hugged her so hard she squeaked.

"*Du hast alle nach Hause gebracht.*" He pushed her far enough back to get a good look at her, then gathered her and her sister and niece into another embrace.

"*Nein, nein,*" Katharina said, once he let her breathe. "*Es ist die Frau, die nach uns kam. Sie sollten ihr oder Gott danken, dass er sie geschickt hat.*"

"*Welche Frau meinst du?*" The big man straightened out of the slight crouch with which he'd wrapped his wife, looking around. Alyse had arrived, sock-footed but otherwise dressed, the waist-length fall of her almost-curly chestnut hair hiding most of her chambray shirt, hastily brushed as clean as possible, just like her jeans; but her belt buckle shone in candlelight a clerk kindled. The knife in her hand offered its own businesslike gleam.

"This woman," Katharina said, switching to English.

"An up-timer," he said after a quick look, and his English flowed as freely as Alyse had heard since the Ring fell. He looked her up, from sock-feet to tousled mane, and down from sturdy shoulders to the blade in her hand and the set of her stance. "Colonel Sherrilyn Maddox?"

"No, sir. Alyse." Alyse relaxed very slightly. "Alyse Ballentine."

"You are not the West Virginia teacher turned—*was ist die Wort*...Co mmander?"

"No, sir." She couldn't help the little grin that lifted her mouth. She'd met, one time or another, most of the Wrecking Crew. Being taken for a member *should* have felt like a compliment. "You're thinkin' of Harry Lefferts' outfit—commandos, they call themselves. I'm just a horse trainer."

He pulled his wife close again. "Not from Grantville."

"Originally, no," Alyse confessed.

"What are you doing here?"

Long story, she thought but didn't say. "Bringin' home horses we had stolen. Happens the four of us've been travelin' together 'til these ladies're home safe."

"And how do you come to be holding a knife?"

She shrugged. "No gun."

His eyes narrowed. "You can shoot?"

"I'm from Texas," she replied.

"When we traveled to Grantville for Katharina to teach and learn at the nursing school, we see the Westerns on the Higgins Hotel's"—and he made sure to say it carefully—"television." His eyes narrowed and he added, "Are you a Texas Ranger? We have seen..." He hunted for a word. "Teevee series, like *Walker, Texas Ranger.*"

Her eyebrows, he decided, could carry on a conversation all by themselves.

"More Wade Harper than Cordell Walker," she answered almost cheerfully, the knife tucking itself out of sight. She offered her right hand for a shake. He decided to take the time to find out what she had referred to. "No, I don't have a badge any more'n a gun."

Did her voice carry a wistful note there?

He looked at her again: sturdy, stout but limber, seeing a touch of grace in the way she moved, a handful of respect in the way she spoke, but no shortage of pride and no doubt she could, if need be, take care of herself with enough left over for anybody who needed her help. He nodded. "I thank you for your care of my family."

Those blue-green eyes flashed in the light. "Any time. It's me should be thanking them, *de verdad*, for their help with my horses and that bunch of good-for-nothing horse thieves," and terribly quietly she added, "mostly for not killin' said horse thieves over mistreatin' these ladies."

"Yet," Margueretha said just as quietly, nothing soft about it.

The constable felt the faintest of chills down his spine. His sister-in-law, he realized, had started soaking up the Texan's attitude, seeing the quick look Alyse sent and the tiny nod Margueretha gave back.

He took the proffered hand. "Christoph Müller. Constable."

"Lawman." She didn't ask. "You'll need to know. There's more to this outfit than we brought in. Harder men, better weapons. About a day and a half back, they did us the favor of havin' a falling out amongst thieves."

He didn't even have to think about that. "Stephan," he said, and a man in his mid-twenties appeared as though out of thin air. "You will take statements from my wife, her sister and her niece, and from this,"—he favored Alyse with a half-smile that did in fact touch his eyes—"Texas lady. Find out what these other men looked like, which direction they went."

"Now?" Stephan, clearly, had had a long day—a lot longer than usual—already.

"Now," the constable said. Alyse let herself relax, until a big, meaty paw came down on her right shoulder. "Please, if you will speak first with my *Stellvertreter*?"

Alyse gave him a nod and a steady look. "Get started, then."

Stephan motioned her to follow, walking to the desk and chair with a lamp Müeller borrowed from the innkeeper. Watching her pace quietly along with his deputy, the constable tried not to concentrate on the fit of her Wranglers or the faint strut in her stride. Alyse walked without a sound, and the constable suspected strongly that it didn't depend on sock-feet.

"What is she like?" He asked his wife.

"Like nothing you can imagine," she said. "I think I have never met someone as stubborn as Alyse. Or as practical. She follows a trail like a *jäger*. When one of the thieves in the basement tried to hurt Anna, Alyse came amongst them like...a lioness into a pigpen."

He pulled her into another one of those rib-creaking hugs. "You sound like you admire her." *Admire this half-savage-looking up-timer in a man's clothes?* He wondered if he ought to worry a bit about that.

"She has skills, and character I do find admirable." Had he known Alyse admired Katharina in return, his worry would not have been a faint one, his wife thought with a private smile.

Once all the women had given statements, the constable looked over Stephan's notes. Then he gathered everyone in the room to him. "Tomorrow Stephan and I will go after these men. I have seen these descriptions before. They are a remnant of a mercenary company. I want all of you to go to Grantville, with Alyse. Be seen by a Grantville doctor, and when we transport these men there for trial, I will bring you all home with me."

Katharina opened her mouth.

The constable said firmly, "I said a Grantville doctor, and I meant it. All of you."

"Man sounds that determined," Alyse put in, "sensible woman says, 'yes dear.' Does what he says and then does what needs doin' after that." She turned to the constable. "Which is why you need to get these ladies on to Grantville without me."

He took in her set shoulders, springy stance, glinting eye. "So you can do what?"

"Go with," Alyse answered. "Won't do any good to stop Rutger unless we stop whoever buys the goods he steals."

"All of you said the same thing." The constable ruffled papers. "These men took what they wanted."

"Without any kind of fight. Like Rutger and his outfit expected to be met," Alyse confirmed. "Maybe they figured to be paid, maybe somethin' else. I don't know. But for whatever reason..."

"For whatever reason you think you're going with us," the constable said in his lawman's voice. "Think again. If I have to take you back to Grantville in irons before I can pursue these men, I will."

Any other woman he'd ever known in his life would have been intimidated; most, including his wife, in tears at such a prospect. Alyse stood perfectly still, eyes meeting his, altogether unbothered. Finally he drew in a breath. "Escort them to the doctors there. Safely. As a favor to me."

"Since you ask so politely," she answered with a nearly imperceptible nod, chin tucking slightly. "We'll leave after breakfast unless anybody's got other errands. You sending Rutger and his boys along?"

"I must arrange a wagon and guards." He blew out that breath. "I will send them once that's done."

"These fellows we caught," Alyse said. "They're the ones on the wanted posters in the town square?"

"Some," he answered. Grantville's way of warning about outlaws had come this far within the first year after the Ring fell, though posters outside the SoTF relied on descriptions. Photographs cost money; sketch artists did, too.

"Ladies can use that reward, I 'magine," Alyse said. "Clean clothes. Provisions for the trip. Proper gear."

"And what about you?" He picked out how she hadn't said "we."

"Provisions, I'd appreciate."

Provisions, he said to himself. He wondered what she might mean, and decided he did not need to know.

* * *

For her part, Alyse wished out loud only for groceries; a bandanna—she hadn't seen one here, just like the Smith and Wesson revolver she really wanted, or any kind of cartridge-fed breech-loading repeating rifle—no need to wish out loud for those. It wouldn't help—and a proper laundry, which amounted to another unicorn painted like a rainbow. Margueretha, watching her choose a week's worth of camp food, spoke to Katharina.

"Well, yes, a tailor, and maybe an armorer, too," Katharina said, eyeing the meager assortment Alyse had picked out. By far her biggest parcel contained the grain she'd insisted on for the horses.

"Armorer?"

"My husband thinks you'll want to buy a gun."

"I might, if there were any here I understood," she answered. "What I ought to get's a shirt, and socks, and underthings."

"And you want your—are they Levis?—washed."

She blushed. "Wranglers." A shake of her head and a ghost of a smile. "Doesn't matter. But yes. I'd like to have 'em clean."

"Maybe a change of them?"

"Reckon there's anything in town my size?"

"Won't find out," Katharina deliberately drawled, "without askin'."

"*Hermanita*," Alyse grinned; she might be half a dozen years younger than Katharina, but the woman who'd come into all this as one of three taken suddenly from a peaceful life seemed, sometimes, almost a child by contrast; early modern Germany, Alyse reflected, left some parts of life a lot more wondersome to women, evidently, than did twentieth-century south Texas. "*De verdad*. Where do we go? Who do we ask?"

The storekeeper, properly scandalized, produced some shirts Alyse recognized as the same kind made for the USE Army. None of them would fit the women properly, but all of them could be used as jackets. Alyse found a lace-up loose-fitting pullover shirt and a pair of button-fly USE pants she could trust not to fall off, even if they did stop a full hand above her ankles. Anna and Margueretha chose skorts, as did Katharina. All three of them bought camisoles and blouses as well, while Alyse bought a fat leaf of soap and some knitwear similar to long-johns. The storekeeper looked a little mollified, but only a little. The women headed back to the inn to pack, eat breakfast, and get ready to ride out together.

"Stop here," Katharina said as they passed a stone building halfway down the last block of the town's main street. "There are two or three more things we should buy."

Inside, which proved a cross between a smalltown gun store and a pawn shop, Alyse found her Bowie. She didn't flinch at the price: four *groschen* seemed reasonable, considering the blade hadn't been damaged. Her eye roved over an array of muzzleloader muskets, all with complicated wheel- or match-lock actions; Anna gave a little cry of delight over a beautiful bow, with a quiver bearing a dozen or so of what Alyse's upbringing recognized as bird-points, crafted of metal rather than stone. Fleetingly, the Texan remembered arrowheads made of Pedernales chert and Alibates flint; she ached to show Anna that kind of deadly loveliness.

Margueretha picked up a wicked-looking stiletto and a proper hunting sling, and Katharina added a Suhl-crafted flintlock pistol to their arsenal. They had spent, altogether, a quarter-hour in the place and two-thirds of their remaining cash.

"What do you suppose they'll do with Rutger and the others?"

Alyse thought that over. "Hose 'em off in cold water's how I'd start. After that I guess it's up to the law."

"Cold water?" Anna said.

"In case I had to ride downwind of 'em," Alyse said, and when Katharina had translated the words all four women laughed. Over the next few days they taught Alyse to pronounce a little more early-modern German and she shared some Texas-flavored Spanish with them. They traveled on the schedule of McKenzie's cavalry: a steady loping hour, walk the horses half that long, every third interval get off and walk ten minutes, then rest twenty; all timed with Katharina's nurse's watch. They rested an hour at noon. When they found good water with some daylight left, Alyse pulled them into an early camp.

A quick dip in sun-warmed shallows later, their laundry on sturdy branches, they swapped into clothes bought that morning. Alyse cut a sapling a little thicker than two thumbs, then strung a hook fashioned from a safety pin, stuck a luckless grasshopper on that, and flung the line into the water. She produced, within a few minutes, a fish big enough to feed one of them by itself, then in quick succession four more smaller fish. By then Anna had built a fire. Margueretha cleaned the fish and strung the fillets on branches, and Alyse put a pan of cornbread baked between two of their small skillets from the town's store together. Supper didn't amount to a feast, but put them in a good mood, especially as the German ladies shared a bottle of wine.

Morning after next found them passing Merseburg between daylight and sunrise. No one wanted to stop; the horses remained in good shape. They passed on, Alyse eager to reach country she knew. On the thirteenth morning since she'd first seen Rutger, Alyse found herself looking down the slope into the Ring, the still-sharp cliffs rising to the north and south..

She led her charges by the police station, reporting that she'd recovered the stolen horses. She borrowed a phone to call, first, the office to get her partner's help in putting the school's horses back where they belonged, then the pastor's wife at Mountain Top to let her know she'd be picking up the children from the daycare there as soon as her older kids got out of school.

When Pedro Sebastian arrived, she gratefully handed over eight head of horses; then, one last time, the four women swung into saddles together. Alyse led them down to Leahy Medical Center's new medical annex for women and children where she could turn them over to the admitting desk, and they could converse comfortably with the intake staff.

School bells confirmed the time as Alyse, leading three saddled horses, made her way home. She stripped off tack then rubbed down tired animals, putting out hay, grain, and clean water in the pen beside the pole barn, before heading for her shower. Hot water and soap, shampoo and towels, hadn't felt this good in years. A cup of coffee and a stack of buttered hotcakes with honey later, clad in clean clothes that fit the way she liked, with everything but her hat, boots, and chaps boiling in the wash, Alyse counted out the rest of her share of the reward money. Sixty dollars would cover this month's lights and water, with a few pennies left over.

She murmured a quiet, "*Gracias a Dios, por todos.*"

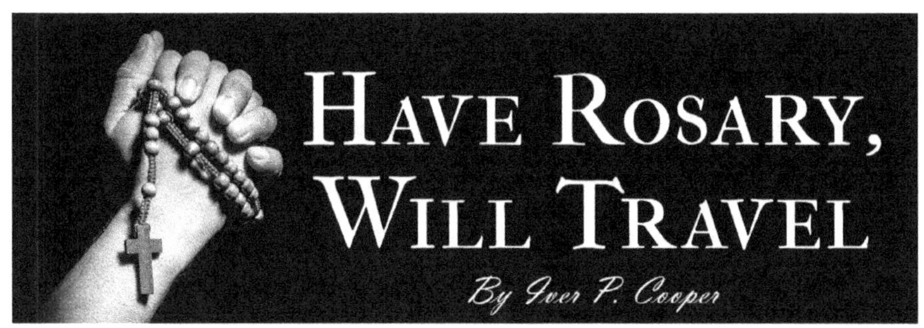

Have Rosary, Will Travel

Iver P. Cooper

Ghent, Kingdom of the Low Countries
1635

Joseph ducked his head as he passed through the trademan's entrance of the stately home to which he had been summoned.

"Wait here," the butler told him. "I will see if the Lady is disposed to see you." His voice capitalized the word "lady."

Joseph nodded. Joseph was accustomed to waiting.

The butler returned. "Come along then...sir." The "sir" was clearly an afterthought, but Joseph appreciated it anyway. It implied that the butler had been advised of his background. Joseph was the scion of an ancient although minor line of nobility that had descended into genteel poverty. This had been the logical result of his ancestors' genius for picking the wrong side in factional disputes (thereby depriving themselves of opportunities to profit from patronage) and making bad investment decisions. But they were good at procreating, hence Joseph's somewhat labored presence on this earth.

Joseph followed the butler up a couple of flights of stairs, and down a long corridor lined with somewhat faded paintings of the Lady's ancestors. But Joseph was in no position to criticize them. They must have made better decisions than his own ancestors, after all.

They halted by a wooden door, upon which the butler knocked. "Baroness, he is here!"

A quavering voice commanded, "Send him in!"

The baroness was lying in bed, wearing a house gown. It was not quite proper for her to be seen that way, but she was undoubtedly past the stage of caring. Besides, the room was already occupied by her maid and, in one corner, a man who, by his dress and manner, was probably her physician. Her pallor suggested that he hadn't been able to improve her condition.

"You know why I summoned you, sir," she declared.

"Yes, milady, your letter was quite detailed."

"And do you accept the commission on the terms I offered?"

Joseph bowed. "I do."

"My butler will give you the advance, and my token. How soon will you be able to leave?"

"The day after tomorrow. I have to see the bishop, and my landlady, and—."

The baroness held up her hand. "I don't need to know the details. Please act as quickly as you can."

Joseph bowed again. "That I will, milady."

Joseph was a respectable man in a not particularly respectable profession.

Joseph was a professional pilgrim. He had been to the Holy Land. He had left his deceased employer's silver urn before the Black Madonna at the

Shrine of Our Lady of Altötting in Bavaria. He had carried a candle in the Marian Procession. He had ridden a donkey on the Camino de Santiago. But never, never before had he been asked to make a proxy pilgrimage to Grantville.

But that was the client's wish, and the client was paying.

Like any other pilgrim, Joseph required the permission of the bishop of his diocese in order to enjoy all the privileges of pilgrimage. Leaving the baroness' home, he noted the position of the sun in the sky. Yes, he should be able to walk to Saint Bavo's Cathedral, see the bishop, and make it back home before dark.

* * *

"Grantville, eh?" said the Bishop of Ghent, Anthonius Triest.

"That's what the lady wants," said Joseph.

The bishop thought for a moment. "I will give you a letter of commendation, but rather than specifically mentioning Grantville as your destination, it will speak of 'diverse holy sites in Europe.'"

"That would work for me."

"And it will keep us both out of trouble," said the bishop. "The Church's attitude toward Grantville is...in flux."

"I appreciate that," said Joseph.

"By the way...." His Excellency blinked his eyes rapidly. "Since you are going to Grantville...Perhaps you can do me a favor. The artists Peter Paul Rubens and Anthony van Dyck are dear friends of mine. I have heard rumors that there are books of their artwork in Grantville. Even of works"—his voice fell to a whisper—"they haven't painted yet. I would like you to buy those books, if you can find them, on my behalf."

"Of course, your Excellency. If you tell me what you are willing to spend and advance the money, I will do my utmost to find them."

* * *

By the time Joseph reached the street of his lodging, it was half in shadow. He entered the foyer and knocked on his landlady's door.

After a few minutes, she opened the door. "I still can't do anything about the noise from the floor below you, if that's what you're calling about."

"That's of less concern to me now than it was when I spoke to you last," said Joseph.

"Going on pilgrimage again, eh?"

Joseph nodded.

"For how long?"

"Two months," said Joseph. "Three at the most."

"You'll have to either pay the full rent in advance, or move out."

"What if I find someone to sublet it for the period I'll be away?"

"That's fine, if the person is of good character and you get the full rent in advance and turn it over to me."

"I'll try. But if I can't, I hope that you can store my belongings according to our usual arrangement. With advance payment, of course."

"Humph. I suppose. Where is it you are gallivanting off to, anyway?"

"Grantville."

"Grantville! I have heard very strange things about that place."

"Well, my patron believes that its arrival was a miracle on a scale that has not been seen since Biblical times."

"I see. I don't suppose you could bring something back for me, as a memento."

Joseph fought back a wince. "I suppose. If it's small and light." And cheap, he added mentally.

* * *

The next day was a Sunday, and Joseph's parish priest, after hearing his confession, and studying the bishop's letter of commendation, brought him before the congregation and called him to God's service as a pilgrim.

The priest blessed him, calling upon the angel Raphael to conduct him safely to his destination and back home. The priest sprinkled holy water over Joseph, his pilgrim staff, and his satchel.

"So, where are you pilgrimaging?" asked the priest. "The bishop's letter was pretty vague."

"Aachen, for sure."

"Ah, the Marienschrein! They have St. Mary's robe, Jesus' swaddling clothes, and the loincloth he wore on the cross, and---."

"And the cloth John the Baptist's head was wrapped in," said Joseph.

"Yes, of course, you're a professional pilgrim, you probably know where every relic is stored or on display. But the letter indicated you would be away for several months, and Aachen isn't that far away...." The priest raised his eyebrow.

"I will also go to the Shrine of the Three Magi, in Cologne."

"An excellent idea, and then..."

Joseph raised his eyes heavenward. "I will let the Lord guide me." And, he thought, I will let the baroness pay me by the mile.

"Well, be careful. Aachen and Cologne are now part of this cursed United States of Europe, ruled by Satan's earthly representative, the self-styled 'Emperor' Gustavus Adolphus. Even those holy cities may not be safe for good Catholics."

"Please pray for my safety, Father."

"I will."

* * *

On Monday, the sun rose into a clear blue sky. It was time to start walking. Joseph would have preferred to ride a donkey, but the baroness adhered to the school of thought that believed that a pilgrimage was more pious, and thus more beneficial in the Hereafter, if the pilgrim walked rather than rode.

Joseph was of the opinion that this belief was more common among those who entrusted the pilgrimage to a professional pilgrim rather than relying on their own two feet.

He had thought long and hard about the route. As he had told his parish priest, he would walk east through Aachen and Cologne. Those were towns he knew well. Then southeast to Frankfurt, and northeast to Erfurt, along longstanding trade routes. After that it would get trickier; he'd have to head east to Jena and then follow the Saale upstream. Unless the folks in Erfurt knew of a better route.

Rumor had it that there was something called a railroad that he could take from Erfurt to Grantville, but if he was forbidden by the terms of the proxy agreement to ride a horse-drawn wagon, unless he was sick or injured, he certainly couldn't ride one pulled by one of the up-timers' possibly infernal machines.

In three weeks or so, if he were lucky, he would be in Grantville.

He adjusted his broad-brimmed grey hat—it was as much a symbol of his profession as the staff and satchel, as it bore some of his many souvenir badges from pilgrimage sites—and began trudging toward the city's eastern gate.

* * *

While there was now a road from Erfurt to Grantville, Joseph didn't like what he was told about it, and decided it was better to keep to his original plan and go by way of Jena. On the road from Jena to Grantville, there was plenty of traffic in both directions. While most of it took the form of walkers, horse riders, and mule- or donkey-drawn carts, on one occasion he had to scoot to the edge of the road to allow one of the up-timers' horseless vehicles to pass. It blew its horn repeatedly until the road in front was cleared, and then roared past, straight down the center of the road, belching smoke from the tailpipe. It was traveling, by Joseph's estimation, almost as fast as a horse at a gallop, and it kicked up gravel as it sped past him.

A troop of uniformed riders stopped to question Joseph. Their leader, who said that he was an officer of the "mounted constabulary," asked Joseph where he was from and what his business was in Grantville.

"A professional pilgrim? Making a pilgrimage to Grantville on someone else's behalf?"

That's right," said Joseph. "It's called a proxy pilgrimage. It's perfectly legitimate under canon law."

"How does your patron know you actually went to the pilgrimage site and didn't just sit in the next town over and get drunk?"

Joseph glared at him. "I bring back a token from the pilgrimage site. And, of course, I wouldn't be hired in the first place if I didn't have a reputation for honesty."

The officer raised his hands in a gesture of placation. "Sorry, I didn't mean to suggest that you were dishonest. I just wondered about the safeguards for those hiring proxies."

Joseph executed a brief bow. "I accept your apology."

"You know," said the officer, "you should get a photograph of yourself in front of one of the Grantville landmarks. That would make a great token."

"What is a photograph?"

"It's like a painting, but it can be made very quickly by the up-time arts."

"These arts...They are not, um, infernal in nature...?"

The officer laughed. "Oh, don't believe the nonsense that some of the clergy have been spewing since the Ring of Fire. The photographic process is marvelous, but a triumph of natural philosophy, not of Satanic ritual. In fact...." He rummaged through a pannier attached to his horse's saddle, and came out with a small purse, which he opened.

"Look at this!" He held a black-and-white print showing the officer and what was certainly his wife and child. They stood in front of a building with large glass windows, which itself was something of a surprise for Joseph.

"Where are the landmarks?" asked Joseph. "And how do I arrange to be photographed in front of them?"

The officer rubbed his chin. "Well you could go to the library to get an 'attractions' map of Grantville, and hire a photographer. Or you could go talk to the people at Ring of Fire Experience. They have a booth by this very road, where it crosses into the Ring of Fire."

"Ring of Fire Experience?"

"That's right. We call the event that brought Grantville to its current place and time the Ring of Fire, because when it happened, the horizon appeared to light up. Ring of Fire Experience gives guided tours of Grantville, and they have their own photographers. So it is what the up-timers call a 'one-stop shop.'"

* * *

It was obvious when Joseph crossed the boundary of the famous, or infamous, Ring of Fire into Grantville: the road within Grantville was paved. And not paved with cobblestones, like the better streets of Ghent, but with a smooth black material that looked like it might be a mixture of crushed rock and tar. It was better even than a Roman road, and that was saying a lot.

Joseph found the Ring of Fire Experience booth without any difficulty and was greeted by a bright-eyed young lady. "Hello, good sir, welcome to Grantville and to the Ring of Fire Experience. We are a company devoted to serving the tourists and pilgrims visiting the Ring of Fire area. Is this your first time here?"

"It is."

"How may I help you?"

"I would like to bring home a photograph of me taken in front of one of the landmarks of Grantville. Preferably a landmark that anyone looking at the photo would immediately say, oh, that must have been taken in Grantville."

"I see...Was there any particular landmark you had in mind?"

"Not really. But I was told I could hire a photographer to go with me to one of them."

"Hiring your own photographer would be quite expensive. I think your best bet would be to take one of our group tours. We have a photographer escort the group and take photos at each stop. It is less expensive because everyone in the group is sharing the cost of the photographer and the guide."

"And how much is the group tour? And the photographs?"

She told him. Joseph grimaced—the advance from his client would cover it, as well as a few days' stay, but he had hoped to have more money left over, since he would have gotten to keep it. Nonetheless, it seemed his best option, so he agreed.

"Very good, I just need a deposit of half the tour price...." The booth lady held out her hand, and Joseph counted out the coins, one by one. She carefully examined each one.

"You are from the Low Countries, I see."

"Yes, I am."

"What is your name and occupation?"

Joseph told her.

"A professional pilgrim? How interesting! That means you make pilgrimages on behalf of others?"

"That's right."

"Then perhaps this will not be your only visit to Grantville."

"Perhaps not."

"And where are you staying?"

"I don't know yet."

"Well it so happens that we have a partnership with one of the inns. Just show them your ticket, and you will get a discount on both food and lodging! I will give you a map so you know how to find them."

"Thank you. Oh, one more thing. Is there a Catholic church in Grantville?"

* * *

After the strangeness of Grantville's streets, it was a relief to enter St. Mary's. It was, albeit downtown, an enclave of the familiar. It was a yellow stone building in the familiar Romanesque style, with two copper-topped bell towers fronting the entrance, and stained glass windows illuminating the nave. Not that it was entirely lacking in futuristic elements. There were, for example, electric lights, although those were not on at this time of day.

The priest was not available, but Joseph spoke to the parish secretary. She promised to have the priest say a prayer on the baroness' behalf and bless the token.

"Come back for it tomorrow afternoon," she said.

* * *

The tour took Joseph and his fellow tourists to see many attractions, including the power plant, the high school, the public library, Schwarza Falls, the Ring Cliffs, and one of the Ring Lakes. Joseph's favorite landmark, however, was the Freedom Arches where the first Committee of Correspondence had met.

The last stop on the tour was a gift shop and Joseph bought his landlady a peculiar artifact that took the form of a glass globe enclosing a miniature model of Grantville, with the Ring of Fire marked in red around it. The globe was filled with water and when he shook it, flakes of "snow" appeared to fall. They put it in a box, with straw packed around it.

Joseph ate lunch at the Thuringen Gardens (there was another discount offer for that) and then went to St. Mary's to collect the blessed token (and to pray that the glass globe would not break during the journey home). He was disappointed not to meet the priest, but so be it. He did get a recommendation as to a bookstore that might have one of the art books that his bishop wanted.

* * *

The books that the bookseller called "coffee table books" were very large and very expensive. And even those that weren't did not include a single seventeenth-century artist. Joseph asked the bookseller for advice.

He wasn't optimistic. "We have carried up-time books on seventeenth-century artists, but we sold out last year. As you can imagine, there was great interest in them. I don't suppose I could interest you in one of the impressionists? Or in Picasso?"

"Sorry, but no. It's not for me, it's to fulfill a specific request from someone important back home."

"Well, all is not lost. Now that we have photography, it's only a matter of time before one of those books is duplicated and readily available."

Joseph sighed. "But time is what I don't have. I need to leave Grantville within the week or I will run out of money. This is an expensive place to stay."

He thought further about his options. He didn't want to return to the bishop empty-handed, but neither did he want to spend the bishop's money on the wrong art book. The bishop might accept it grudgingly, or insist that Joseph keep the book and return his money.

Of course, in the latter case, Joseph could try to resell the book himself. Hopefully, the bishop would at least give Joseph a grace period in which to come up with the money.

"What do you have that is inexpensive, and might appeal to downtimers in Belgium?"

Joseph finally walked out with a children's book on great artists.

* * *

The next day, Joseph went back to the Ring of Fire Experience store to check out the photos. There were several he liked, but he chose one in which he was standing in front of the Freedom Arches, with his arms curved above his head to mimic it. He bought two prints, one for the baroness, and the other for himself.

And now it was time to head home.

* * *

The journey home was uneventful. He delivered the photo to the baroness, and she gave him permission to sleep in her stables until he could recover his room.

He then went to see his landlady, and handed her the box containing the snow globe. She unpacked it and gave it a shake.

"There, Madam! Winter in Grantville!" he announced.

She was delighted, and told him that he could have his own room back in three days.

He had one more visit to make. One he did not look forward to.

A half hour later, he stood before St. Bavo's Cathedral. He took a deep breath, and went inside, and, in due course, he was granted an audience with the bishop.

Joseph explained that he had searched high and low for books on Rubens and van Dyck, but none were for sale at any price. "No doubt because their work is so greatly valued.

"But I did not wish to disappoint you, your Grace, and I thought that you would find this work of interest." He took a deep breath and handed over the book.

The bishop opened it. "Hmm..." he said. And "hmm" again. "I think I have heard of this Rembrandt fellow. Comes from Leiden. Constantijn Huyghens has spoken highly of him. Moved to Amsterdam a few years ago."

"If you say so, Your Grace."

"This will do, I think. But if you ever go back to Grantville, search again. Do you have a receipt?"

"Here, your Grace. And this is what is left of your advance."

* * *

As his landlady promised, he was able to move back into his own room after a three-day wait. He was soaking his feet in a bucket of water when there was a knock at his door.

"Not now!" he called.

Knock, knock.

"All right, I'm coming!" He dried off his feet and walked to the door. Throwing it open, he saw his landlady, with several gentlemen behind her.

"What can I do for you?" he asked. The words were polite, the tone, not so much.

One of them looked at the others. "We have all heard that you have been to Grantville."

"Yes...."

"And we all have errands we would like you to perform for us there."

"I want a history book, I want to know what happens in the future," said one.

"I hear they have a cure for the plague," said another, quickly crossing himself. "Can you bring that back for me?"

He didn't wait to listen to the third. He shut the door on them as quickly as he could.

That night, he prepared a sign, and hung it on his door. It read, "Have Rosary, Will Travel. Except to Grantville!"

Author's Note

I discovered that the "proxy" or "professional" pilgrim, who I thought was strictly medieval, still existed in Ghent (Belgium) even in the 1650s (see Harline, Miracles at the Jesus Oak: Histories of the Supernatural in Reformation Europe, p. 54). Unfortunately, it was only a passing reference.

In David Carrico's "The Taxman Cometh" (*Grantville Gazette* 61), set in fall 1633, there is reference to a company called Ring of Fire Experience.

At The Mouth Of The Mekong

Garrett W. Vance

The Mekong River

1635

Blom sat at his stateroom's oak table sporting a broad grin, which was not an uncommon expression for the ebullient sea captain. He was with his dearest friends, the Nishioka family, and addressed them in Japanese; his skills in the language were growing daily now that its native speakers surrounded him. He could have used Dutch, which Yoriaki and Momo were both quite fluent in after years of friendship with Blom and from selling their bento lunches to other hungry Dutchmen along the piers of two Indochinese capitals.

For this occasion, Blom spoke in Japanese for one member of the party in particular, the Nishiokas' daughter Hana, who was very much the apple of Uncle Blom's eye! One day she would also know how to speak Dutch, as well as its close cousins English and the various Germanic tongues, but for now she was his best conversation partner as they expanded their vocabulary together.

"*Minna-san*, everyone, I am so happy to have you here with me on Groenvisch, reunited and embarking on our great adventure! Thank you for coming with me. It is very courageous of you, but I well know how brave the Nishioka family is! You do me great honor." Blom followed this with a suitable bow over the tabletop.

"*Iie, tondemo-nai desu!*" Yoriaki replied in the always humble Japanese way. "It is you who honor us!" Momo murmured her agreement and all three bowed, Hana sitting on a highchair hastily constructed by belting a square wooden block to a straight-backed chair.

Blom grinned even wider, his face threatening to split into two, which made Hana laugh aloud.

"Uncle Blom is happy!" she exclaimed. Every bit of affection her newfound Dutch uncle had for her came back to him tenfold; she utterly adored him.

"I am! I am happy because I have such wonderful friends!" he told her, which made her laugh again while her parents smiled with the charming embarrassment that Japanese adults tend to exhibit when they receive praise.

"*Saa*, now, I gathered you here because I have some things for you, some small gifts I brought back for you from Grantville!" He reached down to pull up a leather satchel, which he placed on the table in front of him.

As expected, his announcement of gifts brought on a round of you-shouldn't-have and you-spoil-us-too-much, which Blom blithely ignored.

"Now, now, it's nothing really, they are just small things considering we are headed to their source! Consider them a small taste of things to come.

We shall begin with the ladies. According to Grantville custom it is polite to serve the ladies first!"

This made Yoriaki's eyes widen while Momo laughed aloud.

"Well, it seems these Grantville people must be highly civilized indeed!" she exclaimed.

The adults chuckled along with her while little Hana's eyes never left the satchel, as if she might be able to see what gifts lay within if she only stared at it hard enough. This did not go unnoticed by Blom, who winked at her as he reached in and made a show of groping around in its depths for a few moments while her bright brown eyes followed every movement with the rapturous intensity of a small child expecting a gift.

"*Doko ka nah?* Where could it be?" Blom bent over to poke his nose into the satchel's opening, then pushed his whole face inside much to Hana's squealing delight.

"I can't see anything, it's dark in here!" Blom's muffled voice complained, and Yoriaki and Momo couldn't help but join their daughter in laughter at their boisterous friend's antics.

Blom's red face reappeared, his large sea-blue eyes bulging. Hana laughed so hard her father reached over to steady her lest she fall off her perch.

"I found it! This is for you, my dearest little flower." Blom pulled out an odd-looking object about six inches long. It was smooth and made of an unknown translucent substance that resembled polished stone but seemed to be much lighter. The color was the most amazing shade of bright purple and was filled with tiny flecks of pink that flashed and glittered when they caught the light. It took the Nishiokas a moment to realize that it was a hair comb; half of its length was made up of perfectly formed purple teeth, all of one piece with a round-ended handle.

Blom's long arm carried the comb across the table to Hana who was about to snatch it away when a well-timed hiss from her mother made her freeze. Hana looked at her, to be rewarded with a proud smile and a nod that signaled she could accept the gift.

This time Hana reached out slowly and said, "Thank you, Uncle Blom!" as she gently took the peculiar comb from his large hand. "It's pretty!" she proclaimed as she held it up to the afternoon sunlight streaming through a cabin window. She put it over her eyes so she could gaze through it at a world turned purple and dotted with pink stars.

Blom sat back, a pleased expression on his face as he blew out a sigh of relief. "I am so glad that you like it, Hana-chan, I confess that being a bachelor I have little experience with gifts for small children. Moreover, when I left Grantville I didn't even know you existed, but fortunately, I had brought the comb along to give to..." Blom's face suddenly turned a darker shade of its usual red. "Well, anyway, it is yours now!"

Momo smiled, benignly choosing to pretend she hadn't noticed her friend's momentary discomfiture, but Yoriaki let out an amused snort.

"Yes, one imagines there are other kinds of flowers you tend to during your travels around the world's seas, my still-unattached friend. Perhaps some rare tropical blooms? I would wager there is one in every port!" Yoriaki held the pinky finger of his right hand up and wiggled it about in a way that was somehow lascivious, the hand sign symbolizing a romantic interest.

Blom blushed even harder while Yoriaki earned a sharp elbow to his midriff from Momo, which made him relent but didn't wipe away his teasing look. Blom shrugged in mock defeat. "What can I say? I find myself warmly welcomed everywhere I go! It is my boyish Dutch charm!"

The entire exchange made Momo roll her chestnut-hued eyes in silent protest at the impropriety of men, a trait that seemed to know no borders. Hana was oblivious as she marveled at her new comb's magical properties, wondering how someone had captured the sunset sky and made it solid.

Momo stood up to walk over and stand behind Hana.

"Hana, shall we try your lovely new comb out?" she asked while motioning toward the sparkling item that had traveled through time from a distant future.

Hana hesitated, not wanting to hand her prize over just yet, but she also enjoyed having her hair combed, so she, albeit reluctantly, let her mother take it. Momo couldn't help but hold it up to the light herself. She had seen precious stones that had a similar effect, but none as startling as this—it was truly a wonder. She began to pull it through her child's long, unruly black hair, being careful not to let it hit a painful snag. It worked well on Hana's thick mane, proving its functionality was on a level with its eye-catching beauty.

"Blom-*san*, what is it made of? Is it some kind of coral?" Momo asked as she worked while Hana sat uncharacteristically still, enjoying the attention.

"It's called 'plastic.' You will be seeing a lot of it; there are a great many things made from plastic in Grantville, but they aren't usually as shiny as this comb. They are very busy trying to replicate its manufacture here in our simpler age. I have purchased some interest in that project, perhaps it will bear fruit!"

"*'Poo-rah-su-chi-k'u*,'" all of the Nishiokas said in an attempt to learn the foreign word.

Blom smiled, then said it again more slowly to help them mend their initial mispronunciation.

"Pla-stic."

"*'Poo-rah-su-chi-k'u*.'"

Blom nodded as if satisfied while wincing inwardly at their unconscious mangling of the word. He knew that teaching everyone to speak English was going to be a chore, and had made some preparations.

"Yes, we will all work on that! Now, who is next? Ah, Momo-san!"

Momo bowed graciously, handed the comb back to Hana who immediately went to work on the tangles she could reach herself, then returned to her seat beside her husband.

"I did pick these out with you in mind, Momo!"

Blom produced a Pyrex glass two-cup measuring cup and a ringed tablespoon set.

"These are used by the Americans to measure the proper amount of ingredients to put in their dishes when they are cooking. I know you have your own way of managing that, but I thought it might be useful to familiarize yourself with the American style since you will be running an eatery there!"

He pushed the items across the table while Momo bowed her thanks. "*Doumou arigatou* Blom-*san*! It is very kind of you!"

She picked up each one to study carefully. She could read the Arabic numerals, having learned to do so from the Catholic fathers at school, and quickly understood how the items were used. The cup could be filled with the liquid or powder of choice to the desired level marked on the glass, while the spoons could hold a specific amount of seasoning, dry or liquid.

"Yes, they are very exact! I am sure I can put these to good use," she proclaimed, favoring Blom with the smile that had turned many a man's head in her youth, and had lured her husband away from a warrior's life of glory.

Blom bowed back, immensely gratified that he had pleased his wonderful friend, especially considering the awful experience she had so recently gone through. She wore an egg-shell blue summer kimono with long sleeves, but he could glimpse the garish scars on the backs of her hands and wrists that were still healing, slashed there by the Phnom Penh river pirates' curved blades. Graceful, willowy Momo had been well-trained by her husband after a treacherous night attack in Ayutthaya, and had defended herself admirably during the later battle, sending at least two-score of the scoundrels to their graves.

Blom still felt miserable that it had been his fault for running his mouth off in earshot of the local villains and could only take solace in the fact that he had arrived in the nick of time to prevent Momo's untimely death and kill a few of the bastards himself.

Blom pushed away the memory with a shake of his head, then reached into his bag one last time.

"Let me see, what do we have for the man of the family? You were a hard one to shop for my friend, being a man with few needs, but I think you might make use of this at some point."

He pulled out a smooth, red enameled rectangular object with rounded ends. A squared white cross in a shield was emblazoned on it. The sides seemed to be made of a variety of different silvery metal pieces nested together. Yoriaki stared at it with a fascinated expression, quite unable to ascertain what the thing was meant to do.

"This is a Swiss army knife, a very popular item in the future. Watch this!"

Blom used his forefinger's nail to catch a groove in the side of one of the metal pieces. He pulled on it to produce a small, but effective-looking, knife. Everyone watched with amazement as more metal tools were pulled out. Most were meant for functions unknown, but they did recognize a small saw and a pair of scissors.

"I realize some of the tools are probably unfamiliar to you, but they will make sense when you get to Grantville," Blom said as he folded them all back in, then handed it across the table to Yoriaki, who bowed so deeply over the table he almost banged his head on the oak.

"Thank you so much Blom-*san*, it is a marvelous gift, and a marvel as well! I look forward to learning all of its uses!" Yoriaki said as he spun it around in his hands, then pulled out the corkscrew while wondering what such an odd metal spiral was meant to do!

Blom beamed at his little adopted family, filled with the joy he always found from giving.

"This is just the beginning, my friends. I promise you marvel upon marvel when we reach Grantville, the land from the future!"

The Mouth Of The Mekong River

"Look, Hana! We are at sea now!" Captain Blom told his young charge, who he held in his arms as they stood beside the Groenvisch 's wheel. "Water, water everywhere!" He made a slow turn so the four-year-old apple of his eye could get a good look at the calm vastness of the South China Sea from their position at the Mekong River's mouth. The water here was a muddy tan, but sparkling blue could be seen near the horizon.

"*Okii!* It's big!" The little girl's eyes were wide with wonder, having so far lived all of her young life upstream. It was the first time she had laid her eyes upon the ocean.

"It's deep, too," the Dutch merchant told her in his rapidly improving Japanese.

"How deep, Uncle?" Hana asked, fascinated by the sea's grandeur.

"Well, imagine how tall I am. Now imagine a hundred of me all standing on one another's shoulders!"

Hana laughed at the notion.

"It gets much deeper than that, too. At least by another thousand Bloms!"

One of Blom's crew, Zeeman Gjis, came hurrying up the ladder with an urgent message.

"Captain! *Sea Turtle* is hailing you!"

Blom nodded.

"Momo-*san*, if I may?" he asked as he began to pass little Hana over to her smiling mother. Hana looked disappointed but went willingly. She was always on her best behavior where her beloved Dutch uncle was concerned.

"Yoriaki, would you mind joining me?"

"Of course, Blom-*san*."

The two of them went down the ladder, then followed Gjis across the deck to the starboard rail. Ishida's Red Seal ship *Umigami Maru*, the *Sea Turtle*, had approached *Groenvisch* and was drifting about twenty yards off in the Mekong's slowly fading current.

Ishida stood on his deck, his hand cupped over his eyes against the glare from the bright, sparkling sea. When he saw that Blom and Yoriaki had arrived he waved and called out in Japanese, "I wish to call a meeting of all captains."

Yoriaki translated that to Blom, who had grown fluent enough to get the gist of it.

"Tell him yes. I will signal my uncles, then send a skiff over to get him. Tell him to go ahead and make anchor here, we are far enough out of the way of the river's main channels now."

Yoriaki shouted that back to Ishida, who responded with a businesslike bow before going to prepare.

"It makes sense to have a meeting now that we have left Phnom Penh behind, we departed in such a rush." Blom turned to Gjis, the sailor who had fetched them. "Signal *Vlissengen Tuin* and *Groote Hoop* that we will anchor here and hold a conclave on *Groenvisch*. They probably won't be pleased by the delay and will want us to be on our way down to the Sunda Straight, but they respect Ishida and will do as he requests."

Zeeman Gjis, a bright young man who had sailed with Blom on several journeys, replied with a quick nod and rushed off to do his captain's bidding.

"I know that Ishida speaks very highly of your uncles," Yoriaki said. "Without them, he wouldn't have been able to continue his trade with Ayutthaya since we Japanese are no longer welcome there." A frown came to both men's faces as they recalled just why that was.

"Yes, well, Japanese goods are still welcomed there. It has been a very lucrative arrangement for all of us. We transfer the cargo from our ships to Ishida's Shuinsen Red Seal vessels and up the Menam River it goes."

Blom steeled himself for the meeting ahead. He was very fond of his uncles, they had been good to him, but between the two of them no shred of good humor could be found. If one were to look up the word "dour" in one of those illustrated encyclopedias that the Grantville folk put so much stock in, the entry should include a portrait of his uncles.

"Blom, I met your uncles briefly on the journey from Ayutthaya, but I doubt they would recall me."

"Perhaps they will. Have I ever told you their story? It is a bit of an odd one!"

That made Yoriaki's eyebrows raise. "No, I don't believe you have. Please, do go on."

"Yes, it is an unusual relationship that one does not often find! You might think they were both my father's brothers as we all share the Corneliszoon name, but that is not the case! My uncles, Joost and Merten, met as young men serving together on a merchant ship out of Haarlem and struck up a friendship as shipmates. They were both named Corneliszoon, which they found to be an amusing coincidence, so they referred to each other as brothers.

“After the voyage, they returned together to Haarlem and introduced each other to their families, who were of no relation beyond the name, which is a fairly common one. Merten had a comely younger sister and Joost a younger brother who was a shipwright; when they were introduced, it was love at first sight! Their siblings married, making the two of them actual brothers-in-law!

“Eventually, I came along, and when I was old enough my uncles started training me to eventually inherit the merchant business they formed together, Corneliszoon Maritime Trading Partners. And so, here I am!"

"Such serendipitous relationships are not unheard of in Japan, but that would make an interesting tale in any port I think," Yoriaki told him as they went to make ready for the uncles' imminent arrival.

* * *

Momo went down the steep stairs that were more like a ladder from the pilot deck to the main deck, then turned to help her daughter Hana come down. Her arms were still sore from the wounds she had suffered during the river pirate raid, so her movements were slow and gingerly.

Her physician, the imperturbable and stern Sano-san, had told her what she told all of the warriors to whom she ministered: after a few days of recovery it was necessary to “move it or lose it.” Fortunately, Hana had grown up with a steep stairway because their home in the Nihonmachi of Phnom Penh was built on stilts to protect it from the occasional flooding of the Mekong, so she clambered down without needing much help at all.

"My, aren't you a little monkey?" Momo teased her daughter, who laughed and proclaimed, "Saru de gozaru! I am a monkey!" while scratching her head and making "Uki-Uki" sounds in imitation of the macaques that haunted the edges of the city. Some sailors working nearby broke into merry laughter at her antics, which only served to egg her on. "Uki-Uki!" she called out as she gamboled toward them in a remarkably accurate approximation of a monkey's jerky stride, making them laugh even harder as they pretended to flee and hide.

Momo also laughed aloud, which felt good—it had been rare lately. Most of the Dutchmen who Momo had encountered over the years seemed to be pleasant sorts who delighted in children, except for Blom's uncles, a gloomy pair of old crows indeed!

Momo knew that she had been gloomy herself lately. It was understandable that she had felt subdued since the attack and through the general disarray of preparing for the great journey that followed. Her injuries were severe enough that Sano-*san* had made it clear Momo wasn't to engage in any heavy lifting during the process, so her good friends the Tanaka family made sure that she didn't have to, with all of them pitching in to help the Nishiokas pack up and make ready.

Momo felt truly blessed to have such wonderful friends. Over the years they had grown to be like family. The eldest Tanaka daughter, patient Junko, was Momo's close confidante, and she and the next eldest, vivacious Tamiko, often babysat Hana while Momo was busy operating their popular bento lunch business. Momo had already chosen those two, if they agreed, to help her with the restaurant Blom intended her to open in Grantville. It would be good to have a few close friends she trusted working with her in that strange, new place.

Momo had to admit she had been dreading making the trip since she and her husband decided to join Blom's great adventure. He had been a good friend of theirs back in Ayutthaya and had spearheaded their rescue from the murderous usurper-king Prasat Thong's purge of their enclave. She trusted Blom implicitly and also considered him to be family.

So, this was the second time she and Yoriaki had traveled on their Dutch friend's ship, the sturdy Groenevisch, but this journey was different. Momo realized that even though they were going much farther, leaving Asia altogether, she had grown more at peace with the prospect. This time they weren't fleeing from something, they were going to something by choice: a new life. Momo half-smiled to herself and shrugged. After all, how hard would it be to feed a bunch of hungry foreigners from the future, after fighting off a mob of bloodthirsty river pirates single-handedly? Momo crossed herself, quietly praying to Mother Mary for guidance and strength.

While her mother reflected, Hana was still entertaining the sailors with her monkey business, but came to an abrupt stop as she stared at something coming around the corner of a nearby stack of crates—it was Nebuchadnezzar, the ship's cat! The big mouser was a noble-looking fellow, with thick, chocolate fur, chartreuse green eyes, and a sleek, pantherine demeanor, an old-style Siamese. He strolled along with the confidence of one who was the undisputed master of his domain and didn't notice the tiny human lurking there until it was too late.

"Nebu!" Hana cried out with delight as she grabbed him around his waist with an arm across the bottom and one over the top, then lifted him an inch or two off the deck.

Momo stepped forward, afraid that the enormous and not terribly friendly creature would scratch or bite her overeager daughter, but her fears were quickly allayed.

"Nebu" went completely limp, while stretching out his front and back legs as far as he could before and behind him, then went rigid as a post. This unexpected shift in form and weight made his adoring captor lose her grip, allowing cagey old Nebuchadnezzar to slide swiftly from her arms like a greased pig, then bolt past the still laughing sailors and down into the ship's hold, his solemn charge and domain, a realm of dark shadows and secret nooks and crannies he could disappear into with no hope of discovery.

"Ne..." Left holding empty air, the disappointed four-year-old murmured glumly, a pathetic expression of grief crossing her face like a dark cloud spoiling a sunny day.

The sailors quickly grew concerned for the sad little waif who looked as if she might start to cry any second.

"*Klein meisje!* Don't be so sad!" The sailors cried out to her in a chorus. "He is a grouchy old fellow, no one can touch him but the captain. Don't waste your tears on him!"

Momo thanked them in Dutch, then quickly translated what they said to her daughter as she knelt before her, taking her diminutive hands in hers.

"Momma, why doesn't Nebu like me?" Her voice was very small and freighted with emotion. She was just barely holding herself together, close to tears and beginning to sniffle.

"That's not it! It's not about liking. Nebu is just a little bit afraid of you, Hana!"

There was a pause in the sniffling while Hana sorted that out.

"But why is Nebu afraid of me? I won't hurt him, I never hurt Kaki, just ask Junko and Tomoko! Kaki loves me!" A heavy tear began its slow journey down her elfin cheeks.

Momo nodded her understanding as she went to work gently pulling raven-black strands of now tear-moist hair from her daughter's face and pushing them back into the rest of her unruly mane, wishing for the comb from the future that had been put safely away in their cabin.

"Yes, of course you wouldn't. But Nebu isn't the same as Kaki. First of all, Nebu is a cat, and they have different ways than dogs."

Hana gave her mother an annoyed little frown. "I know that! I am almost five years old now, you know," she announced with injured pride.

Momo stifled a laugh and thought to herself, indeed you are my sweet baby girl. And already just as stubborn as I was at that age. "Of course you do, my nonohana wildflower!"

"The Hiranakas' cat Yuki likes me. She purrs really loud when I pet her."

"Yes, but Yuki is used to being around little children and trusts you. I am pretty sure that you are the first small child that Nebu has ever seen, up close anyway, and he just doesn't know what to make of you yet."

Hana still looked unconvinced, but was listening.

"There are some other things to think of, Hana. Yuki is a family cat, a pet who was raised with lots of people around, just like the Tanakas' dog Kaki. Nebu is a ship's cat, his only master is your uncle, Captain Blom. He's more like one of the crew than a pet, here to do his job of keeping the vermin that sneak aboard from damaging the ship and cargo. Nebu doesn't have time to play, he is busy doing his work, so you can't just run up and grab him!"

Hana nodded soberly, taking in all that her mother was telling her in the soothing voice that always made her feel better.

"*Wakarimashita.* I understand," Hana replied with a little bow. "Uncle Blom likes me a lot. Maybe if Nebu saw that, he would like me, too?" Hana's tone held a note of hope.

"Yes, maybe he would! We have a lot of time ahead of us to find out. What I think you should do is watch how Blom treats Nebu, and try to be like him. Then maybe Nebu will understand that you want to be his friend."

Hana's face brightened considerably. "Thank you, Momma! That's what I will do!" She hugged her mother, who hugged her tightly back, grateful to God that they shared such a wonderful love.

"Well, now, I think we both feel better," Momo proclaimed, her happiness moistening her chestnut brown eyes. "I need to see to some things. Would you mind spending some time with your Tanaka friends?"

Hana sighed a little but understood that her mother was a very important person, and was going to be just as busy at sea as she always had been making bento back in their old house on stilts beside the marshes of the Mekong River.

"All right," she agreed without much reluctance. "It will be nice to see Kaki and Yuki, they always love me!"

"Indeed they do. Kaki loves you because you scratch him behind his pointy ears," Momo began to scratch Hana behind her ears. "And rub his back by his curly tail," which she approximated by tickling Hana just above her tailbone, making her squeal with unbridled joy.

* * *

While Ishida was meeting with his Dutch partners on Groenvisch, which had been designated the flagship of their fleet, his wife Malee, their son Jaran, who was a Buddhist monk, and his nephew and fellow samurai Hiuchi H'lek had come along with him from Umigami Maru, the Sea Turtle, which was anchored nearby.

H'lek's cousin Jaran was there to minister to the small number of Buddhists in the uprooted Nihonmachi population, while his beloved Aunt Malee, his mother's twin who had raised him as her own after Saengdao's murder, went to meet with her lady friends. The young samurai's presence wasn't currently required by the day's dealings so H'lek had nothing to do but wander the decks of the large Dutch merchant ship and enjoy the South China Sea's salty breeze.

It wasn't his first time aboard Groenvisch. She had carried him and what remained of his family from Ayutthaya five years earlier, and would now take them to a new life in distant Europe, a journey he would not make, as he had a mission of his own to fulfill. Rather than brood on the dangerous course that lay ahead of him, H'lek distracted himself by examining the changes that Groenvisch had undergone when in Europe.

H'lek, being a warrior, was most impressed by the new deck guns, gleaming weapons of destruction called carronades. There were two, one on each side of the ship, mounted on swiveling platforms so they could fire in almost any direction, with a rather complex-looking mechanism of gears and a crank that allowed their height to be adjusted as well.

His Uncle Ishida had told H'lek that the weapons, the most advanced the young samurai had ever seen, were based on a design from the 1770s in the future world Grantville had come from. The carronades had been built for use on merchant ships that frequently had pirate problems. They required only a small crew to operate and were lethal over short ranges. H'lek hoped they would prove unnecessary on the voyage his people were undertaking, but admitted that it would be fascinating to see the deadly things in action. Perhaps he would, one day, when his uncle's plans for vengeance came to fruition....

H'lek continued his stroll along the deck, being careful to stay out of the way of the sailors going about their duties. Since the fleet was lying at anchor, things were fairly quiet. The passengers had mostly gathered under tarps set up in the aft where they could enjoy some fresh air and sit in the shade, out of the tropical sunlight that grew increasingly intense as they headed toward the equator. Hiuchi felt a bit left out, thinking of the journey that lay ahead of them. How exciting it would be to see more of the world!

Not paying much attention as he mused on the challenges he would face in Ayutthaya, Hiuchi walked around one of the masts and nearly stumbled into two people kissing in the shadows beneath the massive folded sail. Caught by surprise, Hiuchi froze for a moment while his eyes adjusted to the gloom. He realized the amorous couple were his old friend Tanaka Junko, who he had grown up with in the Nihonmachi of Ayutthaya, and Hachisuka Koji, one of his uncle's recruits from Japan, a very promising young warrior. Embarrassed at barging into such an intimate moment, Hiuchi turned and took a step away.

"Sumimasen. Excuse me," he said over his shoulder as he left the two.

Junko's pleasant voice called out to him.

"H'lek-*chan*! Is that you?"

Hiuchi ducked his head and smiled sheepishly as he turned back. He could see that now the two were standing apart and that Hachisuka looked rather nonplussed by his arrival, as well as a bit pale. Junko was blushing at being discovered, but knowing H'lek as well as she did, it didn't seem to bother her much.

"Junko-*chan*! How are you?"

Hachisuka was a bit surprised that they both used the diminutive chan form of san reserved for close friends and children.

"I'm fine because you are here! It has been a long time, hasn't it?" Junko paused to glance over at her new love and sensed his discomfiture at being discovered by a fellow samurai, his leader's nephew no less. On the spot, she decided that there was no point in trying to hide anything from her old friend and said, "H'lek-*chan*, this is Hachisuka-*san*, one of your uncle's men."

Hachisuka, with a definite blush on his face, snapped into military manners and bowed deeply to H'lek, who was a superior officer.

"Hachisuka Koji *desu*. I am Hachisuka Koji. I apologize for what transpired a moment ago."

This apology elicited a sour look from Junko. They were both old enough for a little kissing, after all, it wasn't like they were doing it out in the open for all to see.

H'lek instantly grasped the situation and let out a friendly laugh before returning the bow.

"I am Hiuchi H'lek. We met briefly when you first arrived in Phnom Penh, and I can assure you Uncle Ishida holds you in high regard; he spoke favorably of your prowess in the fight against the river pirates that I, unfortunately, missed out on."

Hiuchi reached out to give his junior an affable clap on the shoulder as was the custom among samurai when in the company of their comrades in arms .

"I can assure you that there is no need to be so formal with me, Hachisuka-kun, we are off duty and among friends here." H'lek used the honorific kun, which was less formal than san and more formal than chan. Kun was reserved for friendly relations with juniors.

Hachisuka allowed himself a small smile and bowed again with less formality.

"You honor me, Hiuchi-*san*. I am grateful for your kind words and would be proud to call you friend."

"Think nothing of it. It is wonderful to see you two together. You know, Hachisuka-kun, you aren't the first among us to land the prettiest girl around. My uncle Ishida did the same thing when he was a young warrior. Well, Auntie Malee was actually the second prettiest, but only when compared to my late mother Saengdao, who was her twin."

This served to make Junko and Hachisuka both blush. Junko gave H'lek a sisterly sock in the arm and proclaimed, "What an accomplished flatterer you are! I would wager that every girl you talk to is 'the prettiest,' eh, Hiuchi H'lek?"

H'lek laughed again. "You injure me! But it is possible that I resemble that remark."

They all laughed, including the earnest Hachisuka who was much more at ease now that he was fairly sure Hiuchi wouldn't be reporting him to his uncle for fraternizing with the locals, which he had also begun to realize wasn't considered to be a big deal. These more relaxed social attitudes were yet another example of the subtle, but profound, differences between his fellow Japanese back in the homeland and those who had lived all or most of their lives in enclaves abroad.

Now that the initial awkwardness had passed, the three of them were just young people enjoying each other's company. Junko favored her new boyfriend Hachisuka with a reassuring smile but refrained from touching him. This was enough to melt away any last concerns he held and he smiled back in his usual disarming way, much to her delight.

H'lek looked on approvingly. He was a few years their senior and had some experience with the self-consciousness that came hand-in-hand with young romance. In his case, it had sadly never lasted long, and he couldn't help but feel a bit—what? Jealous? No, more wistful, really. He had to admit that he was a lonely young man, and the course he was about to embark on would make him lonelier still, but he kept those feelings from his face, and was the picture of big brotherly affection toward his juniors.

Junko turned to H'lek and asked him "Are you excited about our journey? We sure are!"

Hachisuka nodded his agreement with his newfound love's enthusiasm and asked a question of his own. "Hlek-*san*, do you really think this Grantville place traveled from some future time as they claim?"

H'lek cocked his head in thought for a moment, then answered his fellow samurai's question first.

"Well, my uncle does, and so do his esteemed Dutch partners. Captain Blom and his uncles have been there, and his uncles, a pair of very stolid older gentlemen to be sure, do not seem predisposed to flights of fancy."

He then turned to Junko and gave her a smile that spoke of regret. "Alas, my dear old friend, I will not be making the voyage, at least not on this excursion."

This unexpected news put a disappointed frown on Junko's truly very pretty young face.

"I do hope to join you there at some later date, though," he added in an attempt to cheer up his childhood friend.

"Oh. May I ask what you will be doing if you aren't coming with us? Pardon my forwardness, and only if you don't mind." Junko had lived around the samurai class her entire life and knew it was best not to pry into their business too much, even in the case of a trusted friend. One should only ask questions with caution and not expect much in the way of answers. It was only natural that they were secretive when it came to their military machinations, and H'lek's Uncle Ishida was the commander of a small private army that both young men were very much a part of.

"It's no bother, my friends. I will be traveling to Ayutthaya."

This news startled Junko, widening her eyes with surprise.

Hachisuka had come to Phnom Penh directly and hadn't witnessed the violent expulsion of the Japanese from that other Indochinese capital, but had heard much about it from his fellow warriors. He realized that in the relatively short period he had spent with Junko she had never spoken of it, and he was now curious as to what the Tanaka family's experience, and hers in particular, of that dreadful night had been.

It took a moment for Junko to get her voice back. "But H'lek-*chan, I thought that Japanese were no longer allowed there!"*

"That may be so, but do you forget that I am half Siamese? We are famed for being a beautiful people. Do you think I am a handsome fellow?" he asked her in Siamese, and struck a vainglorious pose to lighten the mood.

"I think you are crazy!" Junko told him and they both laughed while Hachisuka just smiled uncomfortably, not knowing the language.

Still, Junko's curiosity wasn't appeased.

"But H'lek-*chan*, why would you go there?" This time, there was a note of concern in her voice. She had borne witness to the terrible events leading up to it, but she and her family had already been evacuated thanks to their rescuers Ishida and H'lek's samurai father, Hiuchi Tetsuo, before the murder of H'lek's mother took place. Junko knew that tragedy was soon followed by the death of H'lek's father who sacrificed himself while covering their escape, and that it weighed heavily on him still.

H'lek tried to sound nonchalant, but his smile seemed strained around the edges.

"Business," he replied with a shrug.

Junko stepped up close to him to take his hands in the sisterly way she would have done back when they were children. She asked him in a low, worried tone, "What kind of business?"

H'lek squeezed her hands, acknowledging her growing fear for his safety. He shrugged again and simply replied, "The unfinished kind."

His face was somber now, and his voice distant as thoughts of just what that business would entail came to his mind. There would be more bloodshed before it was all over, of that he would make sure, and this time it would be the blood of the unrighteous.

Junko nodded her understanding and gently let his hands go. "I will pray for you," she promised him with a fond smile that failed to mask her profound apprehension for his safety in what now amounted to enemy territory.

"I would like that, Junko-*chan*. Please don't worry so, I will be careful, I promise. After all, I'm going home, am I not? Now, I had best make ready to return to *Umigami Maru*. My uncle's business here on *Groenvisch* will likely be concluding soon, so I should go gather up my auntie and cousin." He smiled again, projecting his usual cocky confidence. "You two, please look after each other in that strange, time-misplaced land. We people of Nihonmachi must stick together! I will see you there one day, it is a promise."

He made a polite bow of leave-taking to them, which they returned deeply to show their great respect.

"I will hold you to that, my friend! Go with God," Junko told him.

"Until next time then, Hiuchi-*san*," Hachisuka said and bowed again.

"Until next time!" H'lek called out with great cheer as he left them in the shade beneath the folded sails.

The young lovers watched him until he vanished under the tarps where the others were escaping the day's heat, passing the time as they waited to set sail from the Mekong's muddy mouth.

After a moment's silence, Hachisuka looked at Junko with a raised eyebrow.

"'H'lek-chan?'" He asked her in a slightly arch tone.

"Aho! Idiot! I've known him all my life, he is an older brother to me." It was Hachisuka's turn to receive a sock on the arm, a Tanaka girl tradition he had painfully come to learn, although her younger sister Tamiko's blows tended to smart more—at just fifteen years of age that one was already a force to be reckoned with. Hachisuka was rather fond of his sweetheart's saucy sibling, but also very careful lest he incur her acerbic wit.

Junko favored him with a coy smile then. "Yakimochi? Is your rice cake burning, Koji? I think you are jealous!" Hachisuka was reminded that Tamiko was not the only Tanaka sister in possession of a scathing wit; fortunately, his new love dealt hers out more sparingly. He laughed with a sheepish expression, then switched to a teasing tone himself.

"Not at all, my sweet, it is my greatest pride to have won the heart of 'the prettiest girl around'! I bask in your beauty, I live to gaze upon your radiance." He pretended to swoon, his eyes blinking back faux tears of utter bliss.

Junko laughed merrily at the show. "Baka! Fool!" She used the light pejorative as a term of endearment as so many lovers tend to do. "Now be quiet and kiss me!"

He did.

* * *

Ishida sat at the old oak table between two of his chief lieutenants, Mori and Inagaki, across from all three of the Corneliszoon family captains, Blom, and his two uncles, Joost and Merten. The Dutchmen all looked very somber. Even Blom, who was usually so cheerful and supportive, looked as if he had just eaten bad fish. Nishioka Yoriaki was placed between the groups at the table's side: an employee of Ishida, but also Blom's closest confidant.

Blom was unanimously supported as being the leader of the expedition despite his relative youth, it being his idea in the first place. He was, therefore, the first to speak up, choosing to do so in slow, measured Dutch, a language that the Japanese contingent was well versed in after many years of doing business with his countrymen. Blom knew that his uncles had some Japanese for the same reason, but, considering the situation, he wanted to make sure they completely understood what it was that Ishida had just asked of them.

"So you want us to wait here for another ship of yours to arrive from Japan?"

Ishida bowed his head across the table, in tandem with his two lieutenants.

"Ja dat is zo." His Dutch was accented, but clear. "I had hoped that the *Ōmizunagidori Maru*, the *Streaked Shearwater* would be here by now, or that we would meet her on the river passage, but it seems she is late. This is not unheard of. I am sure I need not explain the unpredictability inherent in ocean travel to my esteemed partners."

Ishida shrugged and held his palms face up out to his side, a gesture that meant shikata ga nai, "there's nothing to be done." By chance, the Dutch used the same gesture for that sentiment, so everyone understood Ishida's meaning.

Blom's uncles grew even more serious. The two gentlemen were well-known for their humorless demeanor. These were men who lived by the winds and tides. Delays cost money, something Ishida also understood keenly. He continued to explain.

"The *Ōmizunagidori Maru* is carrying a load of materials that would be very useful to our efforts in Grantville, goods that can help us build our new Nihonmachi there. I do not ask this lightly: having that additional cargo with us from the start will be in the best interests of us all.

"It is much safer to travel the long voyage together as a fleet. How can I just leave a message asking my captain to follow after us alone, so far through unknown waters? We must rely on your experience as you guide us to your homeland. I apologize profusely for the inconvenience, and can only assure you it will be well worth our while to wait."

Blom looked to his uncles, who were still very much his seniors in their capacity as the owners of his ship and the directors of their entire family operation. He didn't like what he saw there; their expressions were not pleased, and they had leaned into each other to whisper in the code they had come up with over their long years together—Blom could catch very little of it, but knew it was never a good sign. The elder Corneliszoons were a stubborn pair and infamously short on patience. If they didn't agree to the wait it would be very bad for his plans. He had to think fast.

After a moment of intense beard pulling that made Yoriaki fear his friend would rip his auburn Van Dyke out by its roots, Blom had an idea and broke the uncomfortable silence with it.

"I suggest this. Having worked many years in lucrative partnership with our good friend and associate, the esteemed Heer Ishida, I know that he has always brought us great fortune. Considering the unusual nature of our current joint expedition, I would ask that my honored uncles afford us a few days to give *Ōmizunagidori Maru* a chance to join our fleet. It can only mean greater profits despite the small loss of time.

“Moreover, I suggest we send one of our pinnaces up the coast to meet *Ōmizunagidori Maru*. The pinnace is fast and quite seaworthy for its small size, we often use it to scout for us. Once it finds *Ōmizunagidori Maru* it can then return here to let us know of her imminent arrival. If it can't find her after a few days, then it will return and we can make a new plan from there."

Blom's uncles weren't particularly fond of anyone, except maybe their nephew, although they hardly doted on him, but they did hold Ishida in high regard. He was a man of his word with shrewd business instincts, and had indeed made them a whopping amount of money over their five years of partnership. Their expressions had grown amenable and they were now nodding their assent.

Ishida, also a man who tended to keep his emotions held closely to himself, addressed them again, but an unmistakable tone of relief colored his words.

"I thank my esteemed partners for their forbearance in this matter; their wisdom is well known to us. Heer Blom, I would like to send some of my men along with your pinnace so they can explain the situation to *Ōmizunagidori Maru*'s captain, if that is acceptable to you."

"Of course it is! I will order the pinnace lowered and have it stop to pick your men up from Umigami Maru, then they can all begin their mission!"

The uncles, who had mostly listened quietly throughout the meeting, looked at each other to silently choose who would be the one to speak, the task falling to Merten.

"Six days. We will wait for six days," he proclaimed in his slow, sonorous voice.

Ishida nodded his understanding. "Six days. So it shall be."

* * *

Yoriaki and Blom left the meeting and went looking for Momo and Hana.

"So, what do we do here for six days while we wait?" Yoriaki asked the *Groenevisch*'s captain.

"We teach everyone how to speak English!" Blom replied with a confident grin.

THE BREITENFELD EXTRACTION

By David Hankins

The Breitenfeld Extraction

David Hankins

Saxony

September 1631

Life on the run wasn't glamorous, but everything is better when you're with the woman you love. Dominik and Hildegard were working their way west from Dresden to Grantville. Unfortunately, Benedict Carpzov's hunter was forcing them farther north than they wanted. Much farther.

Apparently, thwarting a megalomaniac's convoluted assassination plot makes him a bit vindictive.

After no fewer than four failed ambushes in two weeks, Dominik and Hildegard were on high alert. Then there was the rat incident in Altenburg...well, best not to think about that. Since then, they had never followed the same road for long, never entered large towns, and never talked to anyone. They had to get out of Saxony. They had to escape Benedict Carpzov's reach.

They trudged down yet another narrow dirt track that wound amongst plowed fields between nameless German villages. Dominik glanced aside at Hildegard. Her blonde hair was secured in its usual crown plait, but wispy strands glimmered in the sunset's golden light, giving the illusion of a true crown. Middle-aged like him, though without the gray hair at the edges, Hildegard was the most beautiful woman Dominik had met in a very long time.

"You're doing it again," she said, leaning down to scoop up a couple of palm-sized rocks.

"Doing what?"

"Looking at me like a lost puppy. You're too old to look like a lost puppy." She pulled her arm back and whipped a rock at a thistle. She missed the head but caught a leaf. Her aim was improving.

A grin cracked Dominik's typically stoic expression. "I'm just glad you found me." He slipped an arm around her waist and kissed the top of her head. After twenty years as a widower, he still couldn't believe he'd found love again. Hildegard grunted but hugged him back before gently extricating herself.

"You should," she said, "be paying attention to the tree line." The field to their left rose sharply up into a tree-lined ridge that was too abrupt to call a hill, too low to call a cliff.

"I've been watching," he said, "and I'm pretty sure neither of those kids is Jäger." They didn't know their pursuer's name, so they'd simply taken to calling him Jäger, the Hunter. "Those two are much too young."

"Three," Hildegard said. "Two boys and a girl. Though the largest boy might be old enough to be called a man. He certainly carries that bow and quiver like an experienced hunter." Her second rock took off the thistle's head.

Dominik grunted. He'd only seen the two younger kids.

"So, what's the plan?" he asked. Most men wouldn't have deferred to their woman, but Dominik wasn't most men. And Hildegard wasn't most women. She was Herr Abrabanel's spymaster in Dresden. Or, rather, former spymaster. They'd left Dresden rather abruptly after getting caught uncovering Carpzov's plot.

"My plan," Hildegard said, pointing her chin toward the village ahead, "is to sleep in a real bed and eat a real, hot dinner. There's a Gasthaus here that, if my sources are correct, serves the best Kürbissuppe this side of Dresden. I've been looking for an excuse to come here for years."

Dominik almost tripped over a divot in the trail. "Wait. Are you telling me that we've been wandering through the hinterlands of Saxony for three weeks so you could try some stranger's *pumpkin soup*? I thought we headed north to throw Jäger off our trail."

"Keep your voice down, love. And you're forgetting rule number fifteen of spycraft." She looked pointedly at him. She'd been training him for months in the art of being a spy, and just because they'd fallen for each other, she saw no reason to stop his education.

Dominik gazed briefly skyward. "Uh, 'Be polite, be professional, but have a plan to kill everybody you meet?' You want to kill the kids?"

Hildegard arched an imperious eyebrow and hitched the strap of her rucksack a little higher. "That's number five."

"Oh. Right. Number fifte..." Dominik gazed skyward again, taking the opportunity to watch the kids scurry along behind the ridge, keeping pace with them. He finally saw the eldest boy, a hard-faced youth who moved like he was born among the trees. He whispered something to the girl, a skinny thing who couldn't be older than seven. She nodded and bolted toward the village. Dominik pretended not to notice. He ran through his mental checklist of Hildegard's Rules of Spycraft.

"Ah, number fifteen: Never do anything for a single purpose," Dominik finally said.

"Precisely." Hildegard nodded sharply. "Just because we're avoiding Carpzov's hunter on our winding way to Grantville doesn't mean we can't also enjoy a good meal or two."

"'Or two'?" Dominik asked as they passed between the village's first ramshackle houses. "We've been eating road rations from your go-bag for three weeks now because you said that villages weren't safe. Not until we got out of Saxony."

Hildegard blushed. She actually blushed, something Dominik had never seen. "A woman needs her comforts. I've lived in a palace for most of my life. Sure, it was the servants' quarters, but that's a far cry from sheltering under a gorse bush in a thunderstorm."

Dominik's eyebrows rose. That was the closest he'd ever heard her come to admitting weakness. He'd enjoyed holding her as they slept under the bushes, bridges, or wherever they found shelter, sharing what warmth they could. The idea of sleeping in an actual bed, though, under an actual roof! That held a strong appeal.

The dirt path between houses turned into uneven cobbles. The long shadows cast by the setting sun felt cool after the hot September day. The village was tiny; no more than twenty houses clustered around a small square that boasted the traditional sprawling Linden tree. The ravages of war were evident. Several houses were burned husks, while others were clearly abandoned. The remainder were boarded up, dark, and decrepit. Dominik might have thought it a ghost town if not for their welcoming committee.

Two men waited for them under the Linden tree, one old and weathered, the other a heavily muscled man in a leather apron whom Dominik assumed was the blacksmith. The girl from the woods hid behind the old man, watching them with an untrusting, blank expression.

Hildegard leaned close as they approached and whispered, "Reminds me of Altenburg."

Dominik grimaced. "I thought we weren't going to talk about the rat incident."

"No, *you* said we weren't going to talk about it. I never agreed to anything." Her smirk was obvious despite the whisper.

Dominik drew a deep breath and reminded himself that he loved her. He tried to forget everything about Altenburg and those damned rats and focused on their welcoming committee. They didn't look very welcoming.

They stopped under the Linden tree, and the blacksmith crossed his thick arms with a glower. "Move along, strangers."

Dominik opened his mouth to charm his way into their good graces, but Hildegard beat him to the punch.

"Is this Flößberg?"

Two matching scowls answered her question.

"Does Frau Gerda still serve her famous Kürbissuppe at the Gasthaus? It's been a long road, and I'm absolutely dying to have something warm and satisfying."

The blacksmith started to bark a sharp negative, but the old man placed a hand on his shoulder.

"Gerda was my wife," he said to Hildegard. Despite the years that had bowed his shoulders, his voice was strong. "How did you know her?"

Hildegard inclined her head in acknowledgement of his loss. "We corresponded from time to time on behalf of a *small* friend of mine." She said the German word for small, *Klein*, with a slight emphasis. Her spy codename was Herr Kleingard, an identity that only Dominik and Hildegard's two sons knew was completely fabricated.

Among her network, however, that name had meaning.

The old farmer's eyes widened. He'd caught her coded reference. "Any friend of Gerda's is a friend of mine. Come, tonight you dine with me. We can share tales of brighter days." The blacksmith's glower reached epic proportions, but he just shook his head and turned away.

The old man led them toward a building that was as dark and decrepit as all the others. Dominik pointedly ignored three more boys he'd seen hiding in the village's deepening shadows.

They'd all kept their bows drawn through the whole encounter.

* * *

Stepping into Flößberg's unmarked Gasthaus was like stepping into another world, a world untouched by war. An ancient bar braced one wall, and a half-dozen tables filled the open floor, all of them filled with locals enjoying dinner and beer. Scattered oil lamps gave the room's ancient, polished wood a warm glow. The furniture boasted intricate hand-carvings of mythical creatures and opulent vineyards. And the best part?

The smell. Bratwurst and Schnitzel, beer and bread and—oh, yes—Kürbissuppe.

Their host caught Dominik's glance at the crackling fireplace. The fire was small, just enough to take the chill off the room. "Dry wood," he said, pointing toward the chimney. "No smoke to attract roving mercenaries or deserters. Best to remain hidden." He gestured to the windows, which were boarded so thoroughly that no hint of light had peeked out.

Hildegard asked, "How long have you been hiding, He...?"

"Where are my manners?" he said and inclined his head. "I am Theodor. And you are?"

"Olga. This is my husband, Franz."

Yes, those were aliases, and no, they weren't married yet. A simple lie was safer than a complicated truth. That was rule number fourteen.

The thrum of conversation, which had dimmed when they entered, rose when they slipped onto tall stools at the bar. However, Dominik could tell that those closest were bending an ear in their direction.

Theodor turned to the girl who had been following them like the proverbial lost puppy. "Kleine Maus, bring our guests two bowls of Kürbissuppe and Brezeln, then get some for yourself."

The girl stared hard at Dominik and Hildegard before giving Theodor the tiniest of curtsies and scurrying into the back room.

Theodor sighed and shook his head. "My granddaughter, Beate. No child should be so serious. She has not been the same since the attack which took her mother from us." He gave Hildegard and Dominik a sad smile and set to pouring beers. "That was two years ago this November. My Gerda was injured trying to save our daughter from the soldiers. She died not long afterward. That's when we boarded up the village. We still see the occasional traveler, mostly relatives seeking escape from their own ravaged villages, but hiding has kept us safe from the brigands who call themselves soldiers."

Dominik exchanged a glance with Hildegard. It was a story that was all too common. It didn't matter who won the battles; the little people always lost. "What about your fields?" he asked.

"We work them when nobody is near. Our young sentries keep us informed, and we hide."

Theodor set two steins on the bar, then raised a third in salute. "To Gerda."

"To Gerda," Dominik and Hildegard echoed, and they all pulled a long draught. It was a Schwarzbier, heavy and nutty, and the best thing Dominik had tasted in weeks.

Then Theodor raised his stein again. "To my Ilse, may she find her way home."

Hildegard's stein froze half-risen. "Your daughter's still alive?"

"Last we knew. She was taken by mercenaries moving north to join Count Tilly's army. Their officer, a man they called Captain Teufel"—Captain Devil, what a name—"came into town itching for a fight. He took a shine to Ilse and ordered his men to take her with them. We fought back, and they killed a dozen farmers and burned half the village. The last time Beate heard her mother's voice was as her screams faded into the distance."

Theodor swallowed a hard lump in his throat and then finished raising his stein. "To Ilse."

"To Ilse," Dominik and Hildegard echoed once more. This time, Dominik's beer came with a bitter aftertaste. This endless war had taken so much from so many who just wanted to live their lives in peace.

As their beer steins thumped back onto the bar, little Beate pushed out of the kitchen with two bowls of thick orange soup in her hands. Between her teeth, she held a wooden plate with two pretzels on it.

"Beate!" Theodor chided, taking the plate. "How many times have I told you? If you can't carry everything, take two trips. You can't present a plate to a guest with your mouth!"

"Sorry, Opa," the girl said, though she didn't sound sorry at all. She reached up and slid the two bowls onto the bar between Dominik and Hildegard. With another perfunctory curtsey and a hard stare at Dominik, she disappeared into the kitchen again.

Theodor pulled a small pitcher of heavy cream from behind the bar and drizzled a slow swirl into the pumpkin soup. Then he sprinkled a handful of dried pumpkin seeds over the top. "Please, enjoy. It's Gerda's family recipe. Our youngest is the cook now, and I think she has a knack for it."

Dominik dipped a spoon and took a tentative taste. Warmth spread through him. The flavor was rich, earthy, and heavenly. His stomach gurgled loudly, demanding more. From Hildegard's groan of pleasure beside him, she felt much the same.

"*Mein Gott,*" she said, sagging happily as though weeks of tension were sloughing off her. "That is amazing. I've been cooking my entire life, and I've *never* made Kürbissuppe like this!" She spooned another mouthful. Dominik was right there with her.

Theodor smiled warmly. "Did I mention it's a *secret* family recipe? Gerda won my heart with her smile and my stomach with her soup!" He chuckled at the memory. Then he turned serious, leaned on the bar, and lowered his voice. "Did Herr Kleingard send you? I don't know what information I can provide, but he's always been more than generous."

Hildegard started to give a small shake of her head, but she paused. "What have you heard of Tilly's forces?"

"Not much. News tends to bypass Flößberg since we boarded up. I know they're north of Leipzig, near Breitenfeld. Another battle is brewing." He spread his hands. "But then, a battle is always brewing somewhere these days."

"Too true," Dominik said, reaching for one of the pretzels. It was fresh and soft and soaked up the Kürbissuppe nicely.

A customer called, and Theodor excused himself. Dominik took another bite of his pretzel and glanced at Hildegard, whose smile had faded into a pensive frown. "You're doing it again," he said.

"Doing what?"

"Looking like a mama goose whose goslings are threatened. That's the same look you had in Altenburg. That look means trouble."

"And what would you do if they took me?" she asked sharply.

"I would fight the devil's own army to rescue you." He took a pull of his beer. Then he took another. "So, we're doing this?"

"We're doing this." Hildegard nodded and tipped her beer stein toward Dominik. "To Ilse."

"To Ilse," Dominik said, clinking mugs. "May we help her find her way home."

* * *

Later, in the room they shared in the Gasthaus attic, they formulated a plan to extract Ilse from Count Tilly's army. Then, while Hildegard gave herself a sponge bath from the washbasin, Dominik returned downstairs for one last beer. Though they were passing as married, and Hildegard was an insatiable flirt, their physical relationship remained proper. Once they reached Grantville and Dominik tracked down a priest, he looked forward to changing that.

He and Theodor sat alone at the bar; everyone else had returned to their boarded-up homes. As he sipped delicious Schwartzbier, Dominik tried to subtly question the old man. Describe Ilse. What did Captain Teufel look like? Was Ilse the type to fight back, or to try and escape quietly? He got good descriptions, and apparently, she'd never been a fighter.

From the old man's countenance, he knew what they were planning. Dominik wasn't as subtle as he thought. But Theodor didn't hold back, telling Dominik everything he could think of that might help. He also didn't charge Dominik for the beer.

* * *

Tilly's army wasn't hard to find. Thirty-five thousand men—give or take a few thousand—tend to leave a mark on the countryside. And that number didn't account for the untold thousands of camp followers supporting the army. But even still, it took Dominik and Hildegard three days to reach the massive force near Breitenfeld. They would have made the distance in a single day if Jäger hadn't found them again. And he hadn't even found them through skill or tracking. It was stupid, blind luck.

Rule number twenty-seven: the only luck you can count on is bad luck.

They were skirting the Störmthaler See south of Leipzig. Traffic was picking up, this close to the city, though most of it flowed south as they trekked north, residents fleeing the city in anticipation of the looting that always followed a victory—regardless of who won.

Dominik was digging through his pack for the pretzels Theodor had given them when Hildegard uttered a sharp curse. His head snapped up.

"What's wrong?"

She pointed with her chin toward the steady stream of people moving south on the road. "Thirty yards ahead. It's *him*."

Dominik scanned the thin crowd, and his jaw clenched. Jäger wasn't trying to hide. He was the only person riding a horse. He was a thin man in his late twenties with long, greasy hair, hunting leathers, and a permanent scowl behind his unkempt beard. A saber graced one hip, a flintlock pistol the other, and a holstered flintlock rifle bounced beside his saddle. From the slump of his shoulders, Dominik wondered if he'd finally given up on finding them.

Then Jäger saw Dominik. He snapped upright in his saddle. An evil smile blossomed on his face, and he drew his saber. With a battle cry, he charged.

Dominik swore. They couldn't outrun him, and Jäger had caught them at exactly the wrong spot on the road. The lake blocked their escape on the right side, and on their left was a thick hedgerow separating the road from an asparagus field. Even if they could burrow through the hedge in time, it wasn't like they could hide among the asparagus.

"Whistle!" Hildegard hissed, scooping up stones from the road.

Right. They'd discussed this contingency after the rat incident. Dominik just hoped their plan worked.

He dug deep into his pack. People yelled and scrambled out of Jäger's way to avoid getting trampled.

Where was it?

Hildegard weighed her stones, each just smaller than her fist. Dominik continued ransacking his pack.

The charger thundered toward them.

There! Dominik's fingers closed on a small, metal dog whistle he'd gotten in Grantville. He brought it to his lips and blew a short burst just as Hildegard threw her first stone.

He didn't hear the whistle, but the horse did. Its head twitched, and then the rock grazed it on the cheek, making its head jerk aside. Jäger yanked it back on course.

Dominik whistled again as the next rock whizzed past the stallion's ear. It bounced harmlessly off Jäger's thigh.

He was almost upon them. Jäger raised his saber to attack.

Their third salvo of sound and stone struck the horse squarely in the forehead. Hildegard's practice had finally paid off. The horse threw its head and jerked aside at the last moment, scraping against the hedge to avoid them.

Dominik and Hildegard both ducked as Jäger swung his saber wildly, still trying to attack while fighting to control his horse.

Hildegard threw her last stone as the stallion flew past. Dominik didn't see if it hit, but he blew his whistle again. And again. And again. Every time the silent whistle sounded, the horse jerked as though it had been hit. Jäger sawed on his reins, cursing the poor horse, but then the beast got the bit between its teeth.

It bolted down the road.

Hildegard sagged, resting her hands on her knees and taking gasping breaths. Dominik continued to blow the whistle until Jäger and his frightened horse had disappeared around the next bend.

"Lord Almighty," Hildegard gasped. "I didn't think that would work."

Dominik stopped blowing and drew his own nerve-wracked breath. His hands were shaking, but he managed a wry smile. "I told you it would. I know horses. I knew how it would react." Before becoming a spy, Dominik had been a coachman. "When are you going to realize that *all* of my ideas are good ideas?"

Hildegard straightened, drew another calming breath, and cocked an eyebrow. "I distinctly recall in Altenburg—"

"No, no." Dominik waved his hands. "We are *not* talking about Altenburg."

Hildegard patted his cheek. "I just wouldn't want you to get a swollen head, that's all. Rule number ninety-six: swollen heads are easier to chop off."

Dominik's brows furrowed. "I...don't remember that one."

"I wrote it just for you, love."

Silence fell upon the road, and Dominik realized that their fellow travelers were staring wide-eyed at him. He carefully palmed the whistle. Seeing the horse react to a silent whistle must have looked like magic.

Hildegard broke the silence, grabbing his arm. "Come on," she said, "through the hedge. Time to run." And run they did.

* * *

That was three days ago. Three days of weaving around small villages, lakes, and crossroads on their way around Leipzig. Three more days of sleeping under bushes and bridges.

Not that Dominik had complained. He was keenly aware of rule number thirty-nine: The shortest distance to an ambush is a straight line. If they couldn't predict their route, how could Jäger?

They approached Count Tilly's army in the pre-dawn darkness. They'd expected to find most everyone still asleep, but the encampment was a hive of activity. There were no sentries at the southern end where the camp followers had set up, so Dominik and Hildegard melted into the commotion. The darkness helped.

The plan was simple. Dominik would pretend to be a courier with a message for Captain Teufel. They'd ask directions, find his tent, deliver a bogus message, see if Ilse was there, and then decide how to extract her. There were, of course, a thousand things that could go wrong, but Hildegard was excellent at improvised solutions. Dominik was happy to let her lead that part of the extraction.

Finding Captain Teufel's tent was not as simple. They wandered for nearly an hour, stumbling in the dark and asking directions with no luck. With only a gibbous moon and other people's torchlight to guide them, they spent half the time tripping over themselves. Most people didn't even notice them in the dark. Everyone was focused on final preparations so the army could form up at dawn.

The Battle of Breitenfeld would happen today.

Finally, they found a farrier who recognized Captain Teufel's name. He pointed north with his hammer before he resumed shaping a horseshoe.

They trudged north through the camp, asking directions until they found a row of officers' tents that were a little more orderly than the others. Captain Teufel's tent was at the end.

Hildegard held back, waiting in the shadows of a tree beside two picketed horses while Dominik approached the tent.

He cleared his throat, trying not to let his nerves show. "Captain Teufel?" he called. "I have a message for you."

There was a moment of silence before a rich baritone barked, "Enter!"

Dominik pushed the flap aside and strode into the torchlit tent. It smelled of sweat and sour beer. Captain Teufel was strapping on his armor beside his cot, cursing at the cringing young woman who was helping him. She matched Theodor's descriptions. They'd found Ilse.

Dominik stepped forward, then froze when a blade pressed against his throat.

A voice from his right side said, "There you are, spy. You've led us on a merry little dance, haven't you? Where's the woman?" Dominik's eyes flicked to the side. Jäger stood beside the tent flap, his saber held steady.

"How'd you find us?" Dominik countered, not even bothering to try bluffing his way out.

"It took a while. I had to track you back to that little shithole Flößberg, but once I got the story out of that old innkeeper, I knew where you were going." He smiled darkly. "And here you are."

Ilse's shoulders hunched at her village's name, and she glanced up, pausing until Teufel cuffed her with a curse.

"Nobody's coming to rescue you, girl. You're mine until you die or I kill you." The mercenary cuffed her again. She hunched her shoulders and resumed strapping on his armor.

Dominik's pulse, already pounding, skipped a beat. "Did Theodor survive the questioning?"

Jäger shrugged. "He'll live. Not that it'll make a difference to your fate. Where's the woman?"

Dominik gulped, but didn't answer.

Teufel glanced up, looking between Dominik and his captor. He grunted. "You have your spy. I believe this concludes our business." He snapped his fingers and held out an open palm. Jäger grimaced but fished out a small purse and flung it over, not taking his gaze off Dominik.

He missed.

Several things happened at once. Teufel lunged for the purse, but it passed through his fingers and hit the ground with a jangle. All eyes naturally glanced down at the sound, even Jäger's. In that split second, Dominik jerked back from the saber and dropped to one knee.

"It's a trap!" he yelled.

At the same time, Ilse did something completely unexpected. She drew Captain Teufel's dagger from the sword belt on his cot and rammed it into the mercenary's armpit with a scream.

Teufel roared with pain, spun, and slammed Ilse with a backhanded blow. She flew over the cot and crashed into the corner pole. It didn't snap, but it popped out of position, collapsing that corner of the tent.

Captain Teufel dropped to his knees. He drew one last gurgling breath before he collapsed with a clatter of armor. He didn't move again.

Dominik scrabbled backwards as Jäger chopped downward. His saber clipped the toes of Dominik's boots as he fled the tent just as Hildegard entered. But while he exited through the door, she entered through the wall behind Jäger, cutting a long slit with her knife. She'd acquired a torch and thrust it in before her. It hit Jäger in the back, right between the shoulders. His leather jerkin didn't burn, but his hair did.

Jäger dropped his sword and spun, yelling as he slapped at his flaming locks.

Hildegard dropped the torch and ducked back out of the tent. She sliced the nearest support rope, then the next. Taking his cue, Dominik drew his knife and did the same on the other side. The tent collapsed with a *whump,* leaving outlines of the cot, field desk, and two men. Then he ran around to where Ilse had fallen. She was pulling herself free of the heavy canvas. The young woman was hyperventilating, babbling to herself.

"Oh god oh god oh god. I killed him. I killed him!"

Dominik squatted down and caught her gaze. He must have looked like a ghost in the gibbous moonlight, his face only barely illuminated by a torch outside the next tent. She froze like a rabbit. "Did he deserve it?" he asked gently.

Her face screwed up in remembered pain, and she nodded.

"Good. Do you want to go home?" He extended his hand.

Tears streamed down Ilse's face as she nodded again. She grabbed his hand and let him pull her free.

Jäger was still under the now-smoldering tent, yelling and cursing as he scrabbled around for an edge.

Hildegard freed the horses from their pickets and swung into the nearest saddle. Her skirts pushed up to her knees. "Ilse, with me," she said, extending a hand. Ilse swung up behind her while Dominik took the other horse. He realized that it was Jäger's and leaned down to pat the stallion's neck. "Sorry about the rocks, boy. I'll make it up to you, I swear."

A handful of soldiers, alerted by the screams, were running toward them down the line of tents. Several officers had their heads poked out of their own tents, asking about the ruckus. But in the near-darkness, nobody could see what was wrong, other than that Teufel's tent had collapsed.

"Let's go," Hildegard said levelly and kicked her horse into a trot away from the soldiers. Dominik followed, and they trotted between tents and campfires for about a minute before Hildegard slowed to a walk. They wound slowly around soldiers and camp followers as if they belonged there.

Ilse, who clung to Hildegard like a lifeline, was still hyperventilating. Tears streaked her face. "Why aren't we running?"

"Dominik?" Hildegard asked in her best schoolteacher's voice.

He answered, keeping his voice low and calm despite the pounding blood in his ears. "Because of rule number twenty: Running attracts attention. It's better if we just fade away into the night."

And that's what they did. As Count Tilly's army prepared for war, Dominik, Hildegard, and Ilse slipped quietly south with the dawn, leaving the encampment behind.

* * *

Jäger wouldn't be following them anytime soon, not without his horse, so they rode directly to Flößberg. The ride from Breitenfeld only took a couple of hours, and they were happy to leave the heavy *crump—crump—crump* of artillery behind.

Hildegard slowed their horses to a walk when they reached Flößberg's surrounding fields, giving the young watchers time to alert the village to their return. They didn't want to catch an arrow out of a misunderstanding.

Theodor and the blacksmith were waiting for them again under the Linden tree, though both were distinctly more battered than the last time Dominik had seen them. In addition to the obvious bruises, the blacksmith's arm was in a sling, and Theodor's forehead was wrapped in a bandage.

Hildegard hadn't even stopped her horse before Ilse slid off with a cry of "Papa!" She ran and wrapped Theodor in a bear hug.

"*Schatzi*! Ach, careful of an old man's ribs!" he said. Yet, despite his protest, he returned the hug just as fiercely. Then Ilse pulled back and looked around.

"Where's Beate?"

The Gasthaus door creaked open, and the little girl stepped tentatively out.

Ilse gasped and knelt, her hands covering her mouth. "Oh, *Meine Kleine Maus*. You've gotten so big."

"Mama?" Beate said. Her stern demeanor cracked. "Mama!" The little girl rushed across the square and tackled her mother in a sobbing hug.

Theodor swiped at his eyes and looked up at Dominik. "I can't thank you enough. Captain Teuf...?"

Dominik shook his head. "He won't be back."

"Good." Theodor nodded his head. "Good."

"But I'm afraid that the man chasing us will. He was waiting for us in Breitenfeld."

The blacksmith rumbled a curse. "Yes. We met him."

"How did he get past your sentries?" Hildegard asked.

Theodor gave a weary headshake. "They were watching the roads. He came through the woods. Took the boys by surprise. I'm sorry. I tried..." His voice cracked. "But he threatened the children. I couldn't—"

Hildegard cut him off gently. "You have nothing to be ashamed of. But when he returns, give him a message from us. Tell him that we're done dancing with him and have gone to Grantville. If he wants to die, he can feel free to join us there. Otherwise, we wish him a short and miserable life in Benedict Carpzov's service."

The blacksmith, who'd remained silent, grunted, smothering a laugh. It was the first smile Dominik had seen on the dour man. "I doubt he'll appreciate that message."

"True," Hildegard said. "But with that, he'll have no more reason to stay here and bother you."

Theodor dipped his head in acknowledgement. "If there's anything you ne..." he said, leaving the offer open. "Well, we'll be in touch with your *little* friend." His voice was fervent. He was now Herr Kleingard's most loyal informant.

Dominik nodded and started to turn his horse away, but Hildegard still had one last question. She looked slightly embarrassed. "When you send your next message, I don't suppose...I mean, I know it's a family secret, but...could you add Gerda's Kürbissuppe recipe?"

Theodor grinned. "Consider it done."

With that, Dominik and Hildegard turned toward Grantville, nudging their horses into an easy canter that ate up the miles. Outside of Flößberg, Hildegard turned to him. "See, that wasn't nearly as bad as Altenburg. You didn't even have to—"

"We're not talking about the rat incident!"

Alice's Place

Bethanne Kim

Note: Alice Blower and her family are historical characters. My apologies for having more than one Alice and more than one Thomasine, but I didn't make up the names, and I can't change them. I did my best to give nicknames to make this easier to read.

Stanstead, Suffolk
May 1633

"Thomas, I'm done." Alice Blower and her husband Thomas had planned to move to Boston with their children as part of something in the future-that-was—but would be no more—called the Great Puritan Migration.

Burrowed under the bedcovers, Thomas's voice was muffled. "What? Alice, what on earth are you talking about? Done with what? I assumed you were done with everything for the day when we got in bed and I refuse to get out from under the covers for anything less than life or death."

"I'm done with England, that's what."

Momentarily panicked by her clear words and icy tone, Thomas looked around to be sure no one could have overheard her. Any tiny shred of tolerance the King had once shown for Puritans evaporated after a new town appeared in Germany in late May 1631. Grantville, formerly of West Virginia, had changed everything. Since Thomas and Alice were in their own bed with the children asleep and she had spoken quietly, it was only a momentary fright. Still, he whispered his own reply. "You cannot say things like that! You know how it is here now."

"Exactly, and 'how it is here now' is a good part of why I want to leave. Things have changed so much in the past two years! Who's to say what it will be like when our children are grown? But that's not the only reason. Losing this last baby was hard on me, harder than I want to admit so don't expect me to say it again. Losing babies, losing mothers for that matter, is part of being a midwife. This wasn't the first and won't be the last, but the way that Martha Haffield has been carrying on, I'm not sure we are safe if we stay here. A friend told me that Martha is talking about complaining to the authorities, again, and not just about my midwifery. If she tells them we are Puritans, I could be stuck with a £100 fine. No one can afford that."

Had she been able to see him, Alice would have been relieved by how grave Thomas' face grew. This was indeed a serious matter. A £100 fine was ruinous. "It sounds like you have been thinking on this. What is it you wish to do, wife?"

The speed of her reply surprised Thomas. Clearly, Alice had given the matter more than a passing thought. "Go to Grantville, then to America, and soon. I am past the danger of the first three months with this child, but I would like to be there before my final months, when travel is more difficult and more dangerous. Even these magical, time-traveling up-timers must need midwives as skilled as me. My mother and I have spoken carefully and in general terms. She also wishes to see Grantville and its miracles, so

I am certain that she will travel with us. It will be a long journey, especially for the children. We will not have help from other families on the ship, as we had expected when we planned to move to America. Her help will ease the travails of traveling a bit." She paused. "And hopefully not add any new ones."

Thomas nodded in understanding. "And, like every other woman in town, you would rather not have Margaret Fuller as your midwife. *Unlike* every other woman in town, you can't use you as your midwife." His acknowledgment of her skill brought a ghost of a smile to Alice's face. Everyone knew childbearing and childbirth was dangerous, but a skilled midwife with good tools made it less so, and Margaret Fuller was neither particularly skilled nor particularly given to spending money on good tools. Worse, she didn't maintain the ones she did have.

"Even so, husband." Alice paused so long before continuing that Thomas started nodding off, thinking she had fallen asleep, leaving him free to follow her. "Even so, I believe it is time for our family to leave this place, husband. The King...Things are getting harder for people like us, not easier. I know that Margaret Fuller is jealous of my skills, Martha Haffield is just plain a misery of a human being, and most women would rather have me attend their births than Margaret. One of these days, a mother I'm helping will die and one of them will see me in court without the warning I've been given this time, and then how will we leave? Who will care for our own little ones? No, I'm done waiting. We need to make a plan and leave."

Wary, Thomas sought to understand his wife's decision. It seemed like more than worries about Martha Haffield was behind it. He didn't know why, but pregnant women and those who had recently been pregnant tended to have moods that changed too quickly for any man to predict. They often seemed surprised by it themselves. "When do you wish to leave and what is the travel route you have in mind? If we are moving, there are things to sell, people to alert, and things to take care of. Preferably without giving the authorities any reason to fear what we are doing. For your mother as well."

"As you well know, my mother sold off most of her goods before Grantville arrived, planning to move to America. As with some of our more politically aware brethren and our own family, she has slowly moved her money into a bank in Amsterdam, leaving only a small amount here. My pregnancy gives us an excuse to travel, as does my sister's. We will say we are taking my mother to visit Anne before travel becomes too difficult for me and so I can help at her childbed."

"Why visit Grantville, Alice? Why not simply go to Amsterdam and then Boston?"

"I doubt even these magicians 'from the future' have anything to teach me, but if they do, I want to learn it before we go to America. And perhaps there will be something *I* can teach *them*. After I am done learning, we will go to Boston, as we had planned, to join our fellow...." Realizing that it might be best not to say, even in the privacy of their own bed, she finished, "Our fellow Englishmen."

Rubbing his wife's back, Thomas spent a few minutes thinking on the matter. "We'll talk about it more tomorrow. This isn't something to be done in one day." Her concerns aired, gentle snores answered him, but now they were his concerns as well and sleep eluded him.

Mid May 1633

"Husband."

"Wife."

Alice smiled into the darkness. "My mother and I had a rather loud disagreement in the market today. It seems she feels I am being a poor sister and causing her to be a poor mother. We must go visit my sister outside London to fix this, and as Tamsin is near to giving birth again, this must happen soon."

Thomas smothered a grin. "Indeed. I am guessing I would be a poor husband and son-in-law if I did not accompany you on a journey of such length, especially in your condition."

"Exactly so. It is well that you understand. Several women who were nearby and overheard decided that if we are going, we could deliver things from them to their families."

"Oookay." Even the King's men had given up thinking that particular American slang was dangerous. Everyone used it. "Any particular women?" Alice named several Puritans they knew, and a few who weren't Puritans but were friendly to their cause. "Ah. I see. They are sending things that travel easily with us."

"Exactly." There was a comfortable pause that lasted long enough for Thomas to start to fall asleep. "I am going to visit Abigail tomorrow. She has some things to send to her cousin, but her chairs are so uncomfortable. If you would be a dear and take a couple of ours over to her house, then I could be comfortable while we visit."

Thomas nearly scowled. "I could swear we are already short two chairs and that I just saw her husband selling hers."

Alice slapped him lightly. "And are we taking them with us? No. But she is sending a warm woolen blanket 'to her cousin' in London. Isabella needs a new bed for her older children. They will have a key and remove this one when we've left. She has given me some fine lace she'll never use. Joan will be taking anything else we leave and is sending a small jug with coins hidden in it."

Thomas sat up with a quick shiver as the blankets fell off his shoulders. "Have you already gotten rid of *all* our things?"

She patted the bed. "It's cold. Lay down. And no, not *all* our things, just most of the ones we don't expect to take. And not your things because I need to know what you want to take."

Snuggling into her back, "I'll have to think on that."

"Think fast. I don't like the way Martha's been looking at me or how much time she's spending with Margaret. Elizabeth Miller heard Martha make some comments about telling the authorities she suspects us to be Puritans. Even before Grantville, that could have led to a ruinous fine from the church. Now?" She shuddered. "Leaving sooner is better. Besides, the kids are excited to see their Aunt Tamsin and cousins in London."

Thomas' deep sigh rippled across Alice's hair. "Two days, if that works for you. It's only supposed to be a short trip so I can arrange things in that time. Joseph can pass his master's exam at any time and has been gradually paying me for the business since we first talked about going to America, so it's nearly his anyway. And yes, the money is in an Amsterdam bank." He took as agreement on the timeline Alice's wriggling into him and pulling his arms tighter around her. The gentle snoring that followed soon after confirmed she wasn't going to argue.

London
One Week Later

When they left Stanstead, Alice and Thomas both told everyone that Alice would be helping her sister deliver her next child, which was true, but everyone guessed they were also taking the rare chance to see the capital before they had another child to care for. By the time they were delivering their seventh child in twice as many years, most women had a good sense of what was normal or not and Tamsin hadn't sent for her sister's help yet. So why else would Alice take her husband and children as well?

Alice, Thomas, their three children (Alice—called Lissie—Sarah, and John), and her mother Thomasine slid, jumped, and shimmied out of a wagon piled high with goods and headed toward the small London home of her sister, also named Thomasine but shortened to Tamsin. Shaking the road dust from their skirts and adjusting their hats, Alice and her mother followed Lissie, Sarah, and John to the door while Thomas stayed to guard the wagon. Eighteen-year-old Lissie was a young lady anxious to show off her manners to her aunt, but also young enough to be excited to see her cousins again. As a result, the knocking started off gentle but soon turned excited.

The door opened on a plump woman wearing an apron speckled with flour. Holding her arms wide, she called, "Welcome to my family who are definitely here for real because this is definitely *not* me teasing my children who can now come and see their cousins live and in person! Also, their aunt, uncle, and grandmother are here!" As her voice carried through the house, the sound of clumping feet started racing toward the front door.

Sarah and John ducked under her arms, looking for their cousins, while Alice, Thomas, and Thomasine all laughed at the silly faces Tamsin was making while Lissie hugged her. Taking a step back, she looked critically at her niece, still holding her hands. "Well now, you've grown quite a bit. You are a proper young lady! As you may have guessed, my children didn't quite believe you were all really coming for a visit, but my Mary will be excited to see you. I left her in the kitchen to make sure the stew doesn't burn.

"As for your cart and horses, Thomas, our neighbor's out of town and you can use his stable for a few days. When he's home, you'll need to find another place. Henry and Edward will help you."

As they settled into the front room, Alice's face grew serious. "Don't lie to me, sister dear. You're trying to pretend and most would believe it, but you're not well." She waved a hand as Tamsin tried to speak. "No, I've been a midwife too long to believe whatever it is you want to tell me. It's nearly time, the child is sideways, and you can feel something isn't right." She leaned back with her arms crossed, daring her sister to deny it.

Wilting into a chair, Tamsin blew out a breath. "Very well. Yes, it feels wrong. And when he kicks, it's in the wrong place. And I saw his little hand pushing out to the side this morning. I know the dangers, but I don't want to worry my family and there's nothing even you can do."

Thomasine snorted. "If anyone can help, it's your sister."

Tamsin shook her head. "No, if anyone could help, it's a physician who calls himself an *accoucheur*—Peter Chamberlen of London. He was there when our beloved Queen gave birth to Charles, so he retains the King's favor. He helps with the hardest childbirths and is said to have saved many, but it's so very expensive. I'll not ruin my family over this." Alice and Thomasine both whistled when she said how much.

After several minutes, Thomasine broke the silence in the room. "Come with us."

Tamsin startled as her mother reached for her hand and her sister nodded along, clearly in complete agreement. "What? What are you talking about and how does that help with my pregnancy?"

Alice spoke first. "You wanted to come to America. If you still want to, sell your things and come with us to Amsterdam. Needing money to pay for the doctor will give you an excuse to sell things you can't bring with you."

Thomasine kept a firm grip on Tamsin's hand, looking her straight in the eye. "Please, at least consider it. You will be there for each other and I will have two of my children to help in my old age." She took a deep breath. "But if you don't want to, I will pay for this Chamberlen person if that's what has to happen to keep you and the little one alive. If I don't have enough to live on in my final years, it will be enough to know that I've kept you alive."

Tamsin dropped her chin and rolled her eyes up to look at her mother. "Seriously? Guilt? That's where you're going already? Before I even have a chance to talk to Edmund? He would also like me alive, you know."

The front door clicked shut and a deep voice joined the conversation. "I would, would I? Are you so sure I'm that fond of you, wife?" Seeing Tamsin start to push out of her chair, Edmund walked over and stopped her, giving her a kiss on the top of her head. "You're right, of course, but what particular danger is your life in right now that I'm not aware of?"

After the three women caught him up, Edmund looked around the room. "We'll sell the table first. It's easy enough to say we'll be buying a new, larger one since that has been too small for years. Then we'll see what else might have a better home." Tamsin started to speak, but Edmund put a finger to her mouth. "No. I'll not hear whatever you have to say. We both know enough women who treat their stepchildren badly."

Thomasine broke in, "You should hear the stories about how Martha Haffield treats her stepchildren. It's a scandal!"

Edmund bit back a smile. "We'll sell what we must to keep you safe." He paused and looked her straight in the eyes before whispering, "And to pay for tickets and warm clothing for us all since it sounds like we'll be going on a sea voyage to somewhere a bit nippier than London." He scowled. "Safer too."

Three Days Later

Thomasine held a cloth to one daughter's forehead as the other shook her head. "It's not going well, Tamsin, you know that. We've waited long enough. The other midwives gave me the address. Mother should go now.

Thomas will go with her since he's got no work just now." Her voice weak, Tamsin tried to protest. "I won't hear any of that. Mother, have Lissie come in to help, then send Henry and Edward to fetch their father. If you only send one, he'll get distracted and not bring him. But we need the money now."

* * *

Edmund looked out the window, blinking in surprise. "I think we've reached an agreement on price, but I need a moment. Those are my boys outside and I'm not sure why." Seeing their father walk out the shop door and stare at them, fists on his hips, the two boys snapped up straight and walked toward him, ignoring the mud all over them. "Were you perhaps sent for me?" They nodded. "And how long have you been playing?"

Adam's apple bobbing, Henry swallowed hard. "I'm not sure, sir. But it can't have been long!"

Edmund looked them up and down, noting some areas with dried mud and others with fresh mud. "It looks like too long. Come inside with me. We clearly need to rush home."

Bursting back through the door, Edmund placed a list on the counter. "These as well. If you are interested in any, let me know and we'll settle on a price. I'll take what you've offered for the other things and pray it's enough to pay the doctor to save my wife and child, to whom I must go *now.*"

Eyes wide, the storekeeper quickly handed over the agreed-upon amount. Like most people, he had been there himself, hoping and praying a woman he loved would live through childbirth and that the child would as well. "Have the boys hold here a moment and I'll look at the list quickly to see what I might want so they can run it back straight away. I'll send my boy with them to pay, bring things back to me, and make sure yours don't wander."

"You've been fair. I trust your boy to get mine home." With that, Edmund began running for his home, heedless of the damage to his shoes and the risk of falling.

* * *

Hands on his thighs as his breathing returned to normal, Edmund saw a man with a gilded wooden box in his front room. The man sat there even as his wife cried out in pain from their bedroom. Edmund held up a bag of coins. "I'm guessing you're waiting for these before you help her?"

The man carefully adjusted his cuffs. "No need for the tone. I will happily leave and go about my business elsewhere if you can't be civil."

Edmund took a calming breath. *Jesus could turn the other cheek. I can bear this man.* "I apologize. My children got lost trying to find me and I'm a bit upset as a result." He handed over the payment.

After counting it, Peter Chamberlen said, "You seem to be a bit short." Edmund brought the rest of the money they had in the house. "Very nearly." Sigh. "I suppose we can set everything up while you find the rest since I am already here, but this is most unusual. Now, everyone except the mother-to-be must leave the room."

The moment Thomasine handed him the rest of his fee from her money, Peter shut the door in her face. The door was still shut when Henry, Edward, and the shopkeeper's boy returned with payment for the rest of the things he was buying. The boy and the purchased items were gone before the door opened.

What felt like hours later to everyone but was probably less than a half hour, Tamsin was propped up in bed holding her new son, Samuel Michael Rice. He had unusual marks on both sides of his head but seemed otherwise healthy, happy, and ready to eat. The odd machine was already boxed and Peter was leaving with his mystery tool. "The afterbirth still needs to be handled. Since you are a midwife, hopefully you can manage that."

Edmund was absorbed in his new baby and wife when Alice gently handed him the child, pointed to the door, and said, "Out. I don't know why those fools left the afterbirth but you know it can't be ignored. So, out until I call for you to bring the boy back in."

Early June

Alice gently stroked her nephew's head. "It's hard to believe those awful marks were on his head when Peter Chamberlen was done."

Edmund looked at his wife, then her sister. "Tamsin, my love, I left my Bible upstairs, would you get it for me, please?" When he heard their bedroom door open, he turned to Alice. His voice had more steel than she had ever heard in it. "Stop it, Alice. I don't care if they hurt your feelings. I don't care if you are mad they won't share their secret or that you hate someone else being better than you at birthing babies safely. Peter Chamberlen saved my wife and son, and your anger is just hurting her. So do what you have to but get over it. *Now*."

He held up a hand as Alice started to speak and he heard Tamsin's tread on the stairs. His voice returned to normal as he spoke, but the steel didn't leave his expression. "Of course, Alice, why would we possibly reconsider? We have arranged for Henry to apprentice in Amsterdam and we all want to see him off before you leave to return home. It's pure luck that the same family has a position for Mary to be in service with them. Ah, my dear! Thank you so much. What is a deacon without a Bible? I was just reassuring your sister that of course we are all going to see our children off and they simply must accompany us."

Tamsin sank into a seat next to a small, well-worn cradle, taking over rocking from her mother. "One week! In one week, our whole life will change with our two oldest gone. And we sold so many things to make room for our larger family not realizing two of them would be leaving so soon. Ah, well, such is life." Back to the door and window, she winked at her family. "And what of all the things you brought to London, sister? Have they found their new homes?"

"It took many visits, and more than a few wrong turns, but they have indeed." Thomas, Alice, and Thomasine had been busy selling things all over London. One or two small pieces at a time, enough to cover small traveling expenses, not enough to look suspicious. Added up, they had a tidy sum that would make starting over in Boston much more comfortable. "Our cart shall be much lighter on the return trip to Stanstead."

London Docks
One Week Later

The family gathered, watching Henry and Mary board the ship headed for Amsterdam. As the captain walked down the gangplank, Alice elbowed Thomas and leaned her head toward him. Sighing, Thomas headed toward the captain. "Begging your pardon, could we see where the young ones will be staying? Their mother just had a baby less than two weeks ago and is a bit..."

The captain dipped his chin. "Say no more, I have children of my own. I have found it's in my best interest to not be near home for a few weeks after each is born." He looked around, shaking his head. "There are quite a few of you, though. I'd rather the rest stay here and wait."

Thomas reached into his pocket, then reached to shake the captain's hand, unsubtly transferring coins in the process. "This may be the only time they see a real ship, much less have a chance to stand on one. We don't live near the sea. I'm sure you can find it in your heart."

The captain waved tiredly and spoke clearly. "Fine, but be sure you are off in time. Once we cast off, we're not stopping until we get to Amsterdam and you'll be responsible for your passage and return if you're not off."

* * *

The family stood at the rails, watching the coast of England fade from view. Edmund turned to the captain. "Thank you. It's a relief to be gone and have us all safe."

"The sea is never safe, Deacon, but I get the meaning. You aren't the first, and likely not the last, we've helped sail from London since things have turned delicate for so many. But it's good policy to keep up the ruse even during the voyage. Makes it easier for the lads. They can complain about the fools on the ship instead of needing to remember what not to say when they are in their cups."

The first mate joined them. "If I'm not speaking out of turn, I have some advice on handling the seasickness."

* * *

Halfway across the Channel, in the middle of the night, light but firm knocking on their door woke Alice. Wrapping a cloak around herself, she cracked the door and looked straight into the ship's surgeon's panicked eyes.

"Please, I understand that you are a midwife of some renown. One of the other passengers, Mistress Susanna Phillips, has need of you."

Alice nodded, eased the door closed, and got the tools of her trade. Taking a minute, she slipped back into her dress, tucked the blankets around Thomas and the children and followed the surgeon to his workspace. As soon as she saw Susanna, Alice sucked in her breath, knowing things weren't going to go well.

Susanna ripped her gaze from her husband to Alice, eyes narrowing into a glare as she watched her expression change. "You've already decided you can't help me, is that it, Puritan?" She hissed the last word.

Alice held up her hands, palms out in a peaceful gesture, tone soothing. "Of course not. I'm going to do all I can to help you, but that doesn't help with my own motion sickness or the kick to the guts my own little one just gave me." She stepped closer, laying her tool bag on a convenient table. Sleeves pushed out of the way, she did a quick, professional examination. "How far along are you?"

Glaring harder, Susanna raised an eyebrow. "Shouldn't you know?"

Before things got worse, William, Susanna's husband, said, "Nearly three months. We married four months ago and her time of the month came but once after that."

"Thank you."

Trying to remove his hand, William made to leave the room. Susanna snarled and held on tighter, "Oh no you don't. I don't know her. She could do something to my baby. *Our* baby."

Alice managed to keep the sigh in her head. She's seen mothers-to-be like this before. Her reputation was good enough, her skills good enough, that they were rarely this cantankerous anymore, but she remembered it well from her early days. "Susanna, I do need the men to step outside while I do some of the exam. William, is it? If you'll just stand outside the door, you can leave it cracked open to hear what is going on."

Mulish, Susanna nonetheless let go of William's hand, watching to be sure the door did stay ajar, her husband barely visible through it.

Exam complete, Alice let the two men back in. As she started to explain her conclusions, Susanna cried out. Alice turned, frozen for just a moment, recognizing that what she had feared was the most likely next step was starting. Susanna was clearly losing the baby.

Half an hour later, everyone was exhausted but Alice wasn't done, and neither was Susanna. "Susanna, you're almost done, but you have to finish now. If you don't push out the afterbirth, you will die just like your baby did. Do you want to do that to your husband? Have him lose his baby and his new wife in the same hour?" Angry, Susanna had no choice, especially since everyone knew you had to push out the afterbirth.

Soon enough, the room was silent except for Susanna's labored breathing. With everything done and Susanna cleaned and cared for, Alice helped rearrange her clothing so she could return to her quarters when she felt ready, then roughly cleaned and packed her tools. Finer cleaning didn't need to be done at the mother's bedside. It prolonged things for no reason. "I wish I could have done more. Normally I would tell you to rest for a few days, but there isn't much we can do anyway, until we dock. Since it was so early, you should be better by the time we reach Amsterdam. Well enough to leave the ship, at least."

With that, Alice returned to her own bed while a subdued William waited with a sullen Susanna until she felt ready to return to theirs. As Alice settled in beside Thomas, he woke enough to whisper questions to her. "Where were you? Did the crew require your midwifery skills?"

"The ship's surgeon asked me to help a woman who was expecting. Susanna Phillips just miscarried. I hate it when that happens. Some women blame me for it, as if anyone else could do better than I do." She sniffed, clearly annoyed at the thought. "It went smoothly enough, for what it was. The afterbirth was all expelled and she'll have enough time to rest before we reach Amsterdam. But she does seem the type to blame me for her misfortune."

Thomas's shrug tugged on their shared blanket. "Well, we won't have to see her again once we reach port, so there's that." Alice snuggled deeper into the blankets, her murmured agreement fading away as she fell asleep.

Amsterdam
Four Days Later

The family was evenly split among not seasick, moderately seasick, and quite ill for the voyage. Since those who weren't affected had to care for those who were, everyone was ready to be back on solid ground when they reached port.

Alice clutched Thomas's arm while Sarah and John stood in front of them, all fully focused on the busy wharf creeping closer by the minute. Lissie was in the cabin below with her brother Morgan and Tamsin and Edmund's youngest ones. A ship's deck was always busy as it approached port and docked. It was no place for small children or those still suffering from seasickness, like Lissie.

Sails furled, lines secure, the boat was docked and the passengers lined up to disembark. The men with families were at the front of the line so they could have first dibs on any carts available to haul their things from the boat to wherever they were going. The captain already had arrangements, of course, for his cargo. Thomas and Edmund had agreed to move their own goods from the ship to a cart instead of paying someone to do it. By the time they finished, it was late afternoon.

When Puritans stopped being able to emigrate directly from England to America safely and easily, Constance and Hugh Ames had agreed that any who came through Amsterdam could expect a few nights of hospitality from them, as well as a place to store their belongings before their journey continued. As her knock echoed inside, Alice heard a voice calling out for someone else to answer the door. When she saw Alice was shocked into silence, Tamsin side-eyed her sister and said, "Hello, Susanna. We didn't expect to see you here. Is the mistress of the house available?"

Barely concealing her hostility, Susanna ushered them in. Hand pressed to her side as if in pain, she slowly climbed the stairs as Constance walked in, wiping her hands on her apron. Blinking, she took in the whole group. "This is a bit more than we normally have space for. Are there more of you?"

Tamsin nodded. "Yes, but not many. Our husbands and sons are outside with our goods. Is there somewhere we might store them?"

"Hugh! Go around front and help these good people store their things." She gestured for them to come inside. "It will be tight, but we always manage. I'm afraid you've all caught me in the middle of making dinner. If you can help, we'll have enough for everyone."

Not moving far from the door, Tamsin said, "We don't want to impose. If you don't have space and can recommend somewhere else, we shall leave immediately."

"Nonsense. You were just on a ship. I'm sure you can sleep in close quarters, that was just my warning that you'll need to be a bit extra cozy with what looks to be three families here."

Alice finally spoke. "I was under the impression that this was a place for Puritans to stay, but on our entire voyage here, the Phillipses certainly gave me every reason to believe they are ardent Anglicans."

Constance turned and stopped. "Yes, they are. And we are small in number, even in places where we may worship freely. We need to do business with others, and part of what we do is arrange for others to work with us when they reach the new world. William is a vintner..."

Alice snapped, interrupting her hostess. "And do you now believe that good Puritans are interested in wine, or that there are no good Puritans in America?"

Constance's eyes flashed. "This is my home. I would appreciate a more respectful tone. Now, as I was trying to say, William is a vintner. These up-timers have a way to use something vintners consider waste to make breads rise without yeast. If we can reach an agreement with him for this, it will benefit us all. Several captains know we are looking for any vintner headed to Boston and send any who appear our way. So the captain on your ship did.

"Obviously, we didn't expect two Puritan families on the same ship, so we already gave them the larger bedroom."

Tamsin elbowed her sister into speaking. "My apologies. Mrs. Phillips and I did not get along well on the ship. I should have had more trust in you. Of course, we understand that the largest room is not available."

Thomasine said, "My husband was a merchant. I understand how important such connections are. Thank you for making them on behalf of those of us who make it to the new colonies."

More relaxed now, Constance motioned for them all to follow her. "If you don't mind my asking, since you will be staying in my home, what happened between you?"

Alice sighed. "Normally I wouldn't discuss the matter, but you are right that we are both staying in your home for at least one night, so you have a right to know. I am a midwife of some skill. During the crossing, she lost her child while I cared for her. With so many of us unwell from seasickness, no one thought anything of her being indisposed. I didn't realize she was expecting until the ship's surgeon came to fetch me in the middle of the night but there was no saving it. She seems to blame me for her loss."

Thomasine stepped back into the conversation. "I'm her mother, but I've lived longer than any of you. She's the best midwife I've known. Her lack of humility is quite unbecoming, but it doesn't make it less true. This was Susanna's first child and she seems to be taking it hard. We will do our best to stay away from her and be gone quickly. I will be going to Grantville with Alice and her family, but Tamsin and her family wish to go directly to the New World. It seems like it may be best for them to go on the first ship. Or possibly the second one, if the Phillips will be on the first."

Relieved, Constance nodded and started directing them to help her with dinner.

Mid July

Alice had spent as much time as she could talking to other midwives in Amsterdam, just as she had in London, teaching them what she knew and seeing if there was anything new she could learn from them. Now, all their travel plans were finally settled and the whole family was ready to set off. Thomasine, Alice, Thomas, Lissie, Sarah, Morgan, and John tucked their smaller items around the merchant's goods in his wagon. The few larger items were going to wait, in storage, until they were ready to follow Tamsin and Edmund to Boston. Following the advice everyone in Amsterdam had given them, Alice, Thomas, and their family were headed to the Rhine with a merchant, then taking a boat up to Frankfurt. From there, they would go to Eisenach, Erfurt, Weimar, Jena, and finally Grantville.

Later in the week, Tamsin and her family were getting on a boat headed to Boston, but their final destination was a bit vague. They were going to Boston and from there to somewhere that tolerated Puritans, where Edmund could make a good living, and they could buy a nice piece of land.

Impatient with the extended farewells, Kiliaen Pelsaert picked up his reins and started heading out of town. Seated beside him, Thomasine helped the younger children and her daughter get into the slow-moving wagon and settled. "If you don't mind my asking, young man, do you have any suggestions on where we can find transport from the Rhine toward Grantville?"

Trusting his team, Kiliaen turned to look at her. "Ma'am? It was my understanding I would be taking you the whole way to Grantville. I have business to conduct there and can find my way around town well enough to get you settled before I leave. If you decide you need the larger items you left stored in Amsterdam, I'll be able to bring those to you as well."

Thomasine patted his arm. "That's a relief. Thank you. That makes things much simpler for us."

Grantville
August 1633

Alice's head was on a swivel. *Kiliaen was right. It's impossible to imagine. How can they afford so much glass? How do they get such large, clear sheets of it? How can they afford to heat houses made of glass?* The more they saw inside the Ring of Fire, the more questions she had. She noticed the large red brick building with several towers and, of course, lots of windows as they passed it. She sniffed in disdain before turning to Thomas. "The papists always spend so much on their ridiculous cathedrals."

Before she could say anything more, Kiliaen pulled the wagon to a stop in front of a three-story building with a solid row of those amazing clear glass windows on the second floor. Hopping down, he said, "Welcome to 'The Inn of the Maddened Queen'! It's not the fanciest place in Grantville, but it's not the cheapest either. You'll probably want to move soon, but it's a good place to stay for a few days and get your bearings. From what you've said, you'll want to talk to some of the doctors and suchlike and several live practically around the corner."

With all their things safely deposited on the porch, Kiliaen tipped his hat and headed downtown to finish his business.

As the widow of a merchant, Thomasine appreciated some of the changes that had come with the up-timers. She and Kiliaen had talked quite a bit during their trip to Grantville, leaving her with a lot of ideas to implement in Boston and giving him some possible new business contacts in England. For her part, Alice kept thinking about the "forceps" an Amsterdam midwife showed her. There hadn't been enough time to learn how to use them, but she very much wanted to get a pair for herself. Something about how they looked felt familiar but she couldn't put her finger on what.

As they settled into their room at the inn, Alice spoke to her mother. "I had no idea Grantville would be so expensive! John and Sarah have already dragged Lissie downstairs to play chess. Thomas, can you go talk to the receptionist about finding rooms somewhere less expensive, since she so graciously offered to help, or would you rather I do it?"

"Why don't we both go downstairs and let your mother rest? I will see how the children are doing at chess while you talk to the receptionist." Knowing and understanding her husband's preference not to talk to a strange woman by himself, Alice turned toward the door and crooked her elbow so he could slip his arm through and accompany her downstairs.

As they reached the bottom of the steps and turned to head toward the children, the receptionist called out to them. "Frau Blower! I must apologize for not giving this note to you earlier. I did not see you were part of this family until you had gone upstairs. Frau Zimmermann left it for us to give you when you arrived."

Alice frowned. "Who is Frau Zimmermann and why would she be leaving a note for me?"

"She works at the Leahy Hospital. They often have people in other places tell them when there is someone they should talk to coming to Grantville, then they leave a note for that person at all the most popular hotels."

As the receptionist handed her the note and prepared to leave, Alice reached out a hand to stop her. "Please, if you don't mind, could you advise me on how to go about finding less expensive rooms for my family? I'm not sure how long we will stay, but almost certainly longer than we can comfortably afford to pay for a hotel."

"My pleasure, but if you don't mind a piece of advice, as I mentioned, I have seen other people receive notes like that when they arrive, and not just from Leahy. It almost always means that someone in town has a job or offer of some sort for them. It might mean leaving town quickly to work somewhere else. It might mean staying in Grantville for an extended period of time. In a few cases, it included housing. Unless you feel strongly about the matter, you should read the note, meet with Frau Zimmermann, and only look into housing after that."

Looking quite surprised, Alice nodded. "Thank you for your advice. We will do as you recommend." *This Grantville does seem to be an unusual kind of town.*

Leahy Medical Center
Two Days Later

Ermagart met Alice at the front desk. "Your reputation precedes you, Frau Blower. Right now, we are going to see Beulah MacDonald. She runs the nursing program here. When we found out you were coming here, Beulah and I had a long conversation about how we might help each other, assuming you want to remain a midwife?" Bemused as well as confused, Alice nodded. "It will be easier all around if we wait to talk more about that until we are with Beulah, but her office is right over here."

As they entered Beulah's office and sat down, Alice's expression was quite serious. "Hello, as I'm sure you have gathered, I am Beulah Mac-

Donald, head of nursing. I planned to dive right into talking about our midwife program and our plans for it, but it looks like you might have another concern I need to address first. Would you mind telling me what has you so concerned?"

Alice paused a moment, not wanting to offend these up-timers before she even found out if they could teach her about the forceps, but unwilling to ignore her concerns. Unsure of how to proceed, she simply dove in. "I mean no offense, and perhaps things are different here, but I am a respectable married Christian woman and I take my midwifery seriously. I have no desire to be affiliated with *nurses*."

Beulah's expression cleared up. "Ah, yes, my apologies. We have run into this before. Nurses where we come from are professionals who adhere to very strict standards. Since I don't have a great deal of time to discuss that with you right now, I would appreciate it if you would simply take my word on the matter for now and others can discuss it with you later, before you commit yourself to anything. Is that acceptable?" Reluctantly, Alice agreed.

Beulah made a note. "Grand! If it helps, Jena went ahead and made me dean at the College of Medicine's new Health Sciences Department for my sins, as they say. I'd appreciate it if you would keep that quiet for now because it's still early days and not public knowledge. Now, please, tell us why you came to Grantville and what you hope to do here."

Alice was on firmer ground now, despite her concern about Beulah's open admission to having sinned. "In England, I was the best midwife in my county. That isn't pride, it is simply true. I lost fewer mothers and fewer babies than any other midwife anywhere near us. My family are Puritans. We had planned to move to America before Grantville arrived, making it much more difficult." These ladies didn't need to know everything, so she skipped the details about Martha Haffield's plan to lodge a complaint.

"Finally, after much discussion and thought, we decided to go to America by way of Amsterdam and Grantville. In Amsterdam, other midwives showed me the forceps you use and said that there are other advances a midwife might learn in Grantville. Before we go to America, I wish to learn as much as I can of these new skills."

Beulah asked, "And is there anything you would like to teach us? Please, don't think we will be angry at you for saying there are things we don't know. As you can tell, Ermagart here is a down-timer like you. She is on staff as an herbalist because you could put all our herbal knowledge on the head of a pin and still have room for angels to dance!" Alice looked shocked. Beulah sighed. "I know, it's embarrassing, honestly. We relied too much on what we called 'modern medicine.' Even just a few decades ago, our grandparents knew a lot of herbal remedies for things we would take a pill for. But please, what do you wish to teach us? Anything?"

Alice paused before answering, afraid she might seem prideful. "As a matter of fact, the women in Amsterdam mentioned your knowledge of herbs is 'shockingly bad' and that you don't have many midwives. This last comment doesn't make sense, but they said you are 'better at cutting babies out than getting them to come out the natural way.'"

"They meant c-sections and it isn't really true, but then again, it isn't entirely wrong, either." Beulah looked at Ermagart, then made a note. "I'm sure you are wondering why we asked you here. Frankly, we agree with the ladies in Amsterdam. We have several midwives, but up-time, most women relied on doctors to deliver our babies. As a result, most of them either aren't as experienced as your midwives or are out of practice. Not all, thankfully, but we definitely need more. Experienced, rusty, or still active and busy when we came back here, all our midwives want to teach the skills we have, like using forceps and sterilizing equipment, to midwives here and now.

"I'm guessing the women in Amsterdam also told you that up-time, men usually delivered babies, and you believed that so unlikely to be true that you didn't want to bring it up. On the other hand, they might not have believed it, so you might not have been told. Either way, it's true. Up-time, most women went to a hospital to have their baby delivered by a doctor called an obstetrician and most of those doctors were men. It wasn't always that way, of course.

"All of that adds up to this: we are starting a teaching and certification program for midwives. It will have two tracks and we are hoping to get it started next year. One track will train new midwives and the other will teach new techniques to experienced midwives. Now, before you get too concerned, the new midwives will need to work with experienced midwives or nurses until they fully prove their skills. We won't be sending anyone out to deliver babies with nothing more than book learning!"

The shock hadn't worn off yet for Alice. "Truly, *men* deliver babies? Regularly? Even when the mother isn't in danger? But *why*?"

Beulah shrugged. "There is up-timer history you don't really need to know involved in it, but I don't think you'll be surprised to know that it also involved men deciding they could make money delivering babies, money women didn't need because any decent, moral woman would have a husband to take care of her financial needs." Alice's sour expression showed she did, indeed, understand. "The other big reason was that in the middle of the last century, people got a real mania for cleanliness and sterility. They decided it wasn't safe to have babies at home because homes couldn't be sterilized the way hospitals can be. In fairness, they weren't always wrong. A sterile environment is definitely better for a lot of things, including birthing babies, but they didn't take into account that sick people are in hospitals. Women and babies ended up getting some of those diseases. Even up-time, midwives and birthing centers, places near hospitals but not part of them, were gaining in popularity in the late '90s, a few years before we came here."

"So, are you asking me to be one of your first students? How much would that cost?"

"Yes, but no, not really. You are highly recommended enough that we would like you to help us design the curriculum and hire staff. You can examine the skills and knowledge of potential teachers to make sure they are good enough. If there is someone you know that would be a good teacher, we welcome your recommendations. The salary isn't much, but a young man named Sam Reed has rather generously offered to let whoever leads this effort live in his home rent-free for a spell. We haven't really defined how long, yet, but you can count on at least a year. There will be other tenants there and Sam himself may stay there, depending on how the military assigns his duties, but it is a good offer. You will have two bedrooms and one of the two bathrooms in the house for the exclusive use of your family. You will also, of course, be taught any skills we want to include in the curriculum that you don't already know, including something called a c-section, which is when a baby is cut out when the birth won't progress any other way. And before you ask, yes, both the mother and the child normally survive. We are hoping you will become one of the first to earn a new certification as a Surgical Midwife. That means you will know how to perform several specific surgeries related to childbirth and women's reproductive needs."

Alice looked stunned. This was beyond a dream. A dream was something one could imagine. This was beyond her imagination. She gathered herself firmly and responded. "Absolutely. I shall have to speak to my family, of course, and learn more of the details, such as how long you expect me to stay here, but I shall never have another opportunity like this."

Beulah beamed. "We call that 'the chance of a lifetime' and I agree with you. Up-time, I was studying for something called a master's degree in midwifery. I wasn't finished, but I have more than a passing knowledge and interest in the subject. What I do *not* have is the years of experience and skill that you do. I have to admit that I was tickled pink when we received a letter telling us that a skilled *English* midwife was headed our way, because that means you can read my textbooks for yourself. I know how hard understanding some of the words will be for you because we have the same problem in reverse, but it will still be easier than if you were trying to read a German text printed in fraktur." Shudder. "We have, of course, had midwives here over the past two years, but it's been hard to find someone with experience who is willing to work with the male doctors for very long." Beulah blew her bangs up. "No, that's not entirely fair. Once they are trained in up-time techniques, they keep getting their own 'chance of a lifetime' and leaving us. So far, none have been fluent in written English, so they haven't wanted to take on this challenge.

"We knew before you arrived that you plan to go to Boston. What we are really, really hoping is that you will stay here long enough for us to get this program set up, and then when you go to Boston, you'll take our materials and train more women there."

Alice blinked. "I—What? I think I'm not understanding."

Ermagart sat up extra straight. "You did not mention Jena, Frau MacDonald!" She turned to look at Alice. "Our last chief midwife left us for the hospital in Jena, but that's not the important part for you. We have started working on a joint medical degree program with the University of Jena. This is where she will be a dean. Nurses and doctors are important to the up-timers, but they are not stopping there. They have many programs that are shorter but produce skilled medical people. Training programs for EMTs—emergency medical technicians, military medics, and midwives, for a start, are being created or refined with the University of Jena. When they are ready, we will share them with Magdeburg, Padua, Vienna, and any other city that desires to have these kinds of training. And we want them to go to North America as well. But we need someone who wants to move there to help us, and midwifery is a good place to start since they don't have enough people for a full medical school. Yet."

At this point, Alice looked pale, even for an Englishwoman. She had certainly heard of the famous medical schools in Padua and Jena. Even for a woman as certain of her own skill and of God's hand in her fortunes as Alice Blower, the thought of developing a new medical program for use in those august institutions was sobering.

Beulah gave Alice a penetrating stare, then turned to Ermagart. "I believe we may have said too much and the poor woman might 'get the vapors' if we aren't careful. Since my next meeting is undoubtedly waiting for me, would you mind taking Mrs. Blower for a walk in your garden? It might be just the ticket to calm her nerves and give you two a chance to chat. Take as much time as you need for the conversation. You know the house she'll live in if she accepts, right? Good. Show her where it is, if you like."

Ermagart smiled. She loved the garden at Sam's house even more than the one at Leahy and never turned down a chance to visit. "Of course. Alice, if you will walk with me, I have been developing an herbal garden here. You truly cannot believe how little these up-timers knew about herbal remedies." She lowered her voice to a whisper. "*They killed all their dandelions because they thought they were weeds!* It's true. And they had all these wonderful herbs and edible plants they knew nothing about in their yards. I found something they called a spice bush. I haven't found any medicinal use for them yet, but they are edible. The house you will be staying in belonged to an old woman named Irene Flannery. She had large spice bushes, as well as quite a few berry bushes, flourishing in her yard, so your family will definitely be able to experiment with them in your kitchen as soon as you move in."

Several volunteers tended to the hospital garden, watering, weeding, and sometimes planting. The residents of the local senior residences, in particular, enjoyed helping out this way when they could. After taking a few minutes to corral and calm her thoughts as she looked around, Alice spoke. "This looks like a wonderful garden. I see a second garden over there. Is it also part of the medicinal garden, or is it a vegetable garden?"

"Vegetable. You would simply not believe how much meat the up-timers eat, left to their preferences. Almost none of them had a vegetable or herb garden worthy of the name, so we have been planting them anywhere we can over the last two years. There is also an herb garden next to the vegetables, just out of view from here, and of course we use that for medicine as well. But it's obviously more convenient to have a small herb garden close to the kitchen."

"Where did all these plants come from?"

"Some are local to Thuringia. Some are local from within the Ring of Fire. Others are gifts from botanical gardens. A few are plants and seed packets Grantville residents bought before the Ring of Fire. The young man whose home you will be living in donated something called a 'Bird of Paradise' with the qualifier that once we have one of our own growing, we need to send the original to the Emperor. Apparently, the plant is originally from South Africa! So, they truly come from all over. The Bird of Paradise doesn't have any medicinal value that we know of, but it certainly is pretty and unusual to look at. Getting back to the garden, is there something you haven't seen that you use in midwifery? What am I saying, of course there is! That's part of why I brought you here. We need you to come up with a list of herbal remedies used in midwifery so we can make sure to grow what is needed, and send it to America."

The two women found a shaded bench near Buffalo Creek and sat. "I will write this list for you. God must truly have guided my family to bring us such an opportunity. No matter the opportunities here, though, we still wish to go to America. I will talk to my husband and my mother, who travels with us, but I do not think I can refuse to do this work. It is too important. And my reasons for coming here were indeed to learn new skills, such as using these forceps, and to teach any that I may have that you do not, although I wasn't sure the up-timers would be interested in anything I know."

"You will be surprised by the things the up-timers are interested in learning. I have some things to take care of, but you are welcome to stay and enjoy the garden for a while. The Inn of the Maddened Queen is almost next door to the middle school. It's quite an impressive building. You should take a moment to think about what it means that these people spent so much time and money to make a building just to educate the children, and not just that one building, either. Not the children of the rich, *all* the children."

Alice blinked hard. "The red brick building with the towers? This is a school? It's not a church building? Not a church school?"

Ermegart laughed. "No, it's most definitely not a church building or church school! Although I think you could argue that if the up-timers had a universal religion, it would be education. If you stay here, all your kids who are five to eighteen will be required to go to school during the day, every day, with a few weeks of vacation in the summer."

Alice paled again. "We have four, soon to be five, children. Even if you pay me well for my services, we don't have that kind of money."

"I've been in Grantville too long, I think. I take so many things for granted already! You don't have to pay for your children to go to school here, only if they finish high school, at eighteen or so, and go to college.

Taxes here don't go to pay for estates for noblemen, or fancy dresses for their wives. They go to pay for schools, and roads, and *reasonable* salaries for government employees. I can see that you're overwhelmed by it all and don't really believe me. Everyone feels the same when they get here. It is a lot. You talk to your husband and your mother. I'll be in my office at two tomorrow afternoon, if you want to stop by then. If you aren't sure yet or that time doesn't work, just let me know what does. The receptionist at the front desk of the hotel will know how to get hold of me for you, and you can ask her questions about what I've told you. I'm sure she's had to answer them before. Well, maybe not the ones about being a midwife, but most of the rest of it. And she'll be able to help you move into Sam's house, if you decide to stay."

Overwhelmed, Alice spontaneously, and uncharacteristically, gave the older woman a hug. "Thank you so much for all the help. I don't know what we have done to earn such rewards from God, but I will pray to Him and try to be worthy."

One Week Later

Alice firmly closed the front door of their new home behind her, the din of her family almost instantly disappearing. *How do their doors do that when they are so thin and light? A heavy oak door in a solid timber wall, I understand that keeping a house quiet, but not these light up-time materials.* Her thoughts continued to wander down similar paths as she walked briskly to the Red Shield offices on Market Street. As with many down-timers, seeing familiar names like "Market Street" and "Water Street" brought a small measure of comfort, knowing that some things never changed.

As she walked through the entrance, a young woman directed Alice down the hall and into a small conference room where several ladies and one older gentleman waited for her, along with two women she sincerely hoped were herbalists, midwives, or other experienced medical practitioners like herself. Talking with nobility about medical practicalities was rarely easy, or productive.

"You must be Mrs. Blower! It is a pleasure to welcome you to the Red Shield! I am Eleanore Jenkins, President of the Red Shield. You will find out that most of the people who work for us are, in fact, volunteers, including myself. We are hiring more people the longer we are here in the 1630s, but we still rely on volunteers a lot.

"Claudette Green, our Secretary, Barbara Reed, and Betty Ruth Snodgrass are all members of the Red Shield. Mrs. Sims, also named Alice, by the way, her husband Dr. Sims, Miss Reed, and Frau Durer are all Red Shield staff."

Alice noted everyone's names, bobbing her head slightly in acknowledgment of each. As Eleanore paused, Alice spoke, "Dr. Sims, what exactly are you a doctor of?"

Surprised by the question, he took a moment before answering. "Medicine. I am a medical doctor, just as my wife here is a medical nurse, and Miss Reed is studying to become a medical nurse. Before you judge too much, when and where we come from, medical nurses are highly skilled professionals, and we aim to make that true here and now as well. Frau Durer is an herbalist who works with us."

"It is a pleasure to meet all of you. I have been asked to help start a training program for midwifery. If you don't mind my bluntness, what am I doing right here, right now? It doesn't sound like you have a need for that, or for me."

Alice Sims answered, a smile in her voice as she patted her husband's hand. "Doctor Sims doesn't always explain things in order, especially when those things aren't medical in nature. The Red Shield does several different things. One, of course, is to provide medical aid, but another, and one we believe is equally—possibly even more—important, is to provide medical training to regular people. Some of those training materials came through with us, many did not. And of course, our needs here and now are very different than they were Before. For nearly the whole two years we have been here, we have been recreating old medical training and designing new classes any time we can, as we find need for it.

"And now, we find there is a need for training in midwifery. Or, to be more accurate, Leahy has decided there is a need for it and asked us to help them. Doctor Sims, Miss Reed, Frau Durer, and I have been running the Red Shield Well Baby Clinic for quite some time now, so we have had more contact with pregnant and newly post-partum mothers than anyone at Leahy, and we've met quite a few midwives along the way. We have also put together the curriculum for several classes including CPR and Stop the Bleed. Those subjects are all much smaller than this, of course, but they still gave us experience creating curriculum. That made us the obvious choice."

"I....see. I was led to understand that you would have something to show me at this meeting?"

Eleanore interrupted. "I hate to interrupt you, Mrs. Blower, but Claudette, Betty Ruth, and I were really only here to meet and welcome you, so we are going to leave before you all get into the meat of your discussion. One last thing I was asked to tell you before I leave. Leahy will send word so you can attend and watch when they have deliveries. The house you are in has a telephone, which someone will demonstrate for you, if they haven't already. The telephone is an easy and fast way for Leahy and others in Grantville, to communicate with you. Everyone especially wants to make sure you see births that use forceps and a c-section. If you have questions, I promise you, I am not the one who can answer them, but I do look forward to seeing you around town and to meeting with you again."

As they went out the door, Grannie B, Barbara Reed, spoke. "I worked as a midwife for a while in my younger days. I am decades out of practice now, but I kept my bag, tucked away in the attic." Krystal picked up the bag from the floor and put it on the table in front of her great-grandmother, opening the top for her. "My tools included a 'pinards horn,' forceps...."

When the meeting ended, Alice's head was spinning with all the new possibilities and tools open to her now. The pinard horn and forceps, in particular, would make her job so much easier, and save so many lives. She couldn't even contemplate what they had told her about the new Women's Center being planned for Leahy.

* * *

Alice stormed into their home, her barely concealed rage a shock to her family. Thomas started to talk to her, but she held up a hand to stop him. As she blew up the stairs to their bedroom, her mother followed, entering the room close behind her and shutting the door behind them both. "Daughter, what could possibly have put you in such a state? You were so looking forward to seeing these 'forceps' in use, especially after being told you will be given a pair for yourself."

Alice turned a steely glare on her mother. "In London, Peter Chamberlen helped when Tamsin almost lost her baby. He saves babies in London when no one else can, for a substantial fee." She was spitting the words out, still furious at the memory of Chamberlen refusing to help her sister until they paid the full fee, then locking everyone else out during the delivery and even blocking Tamsin's view of what they were doing to her body.

Mystified, Thomasine nodded, "Of course, all the midwives had heard tales of him helping *in extremis* with much success. He brings in that box to assist in the delivery but no one can see what is inside or what they do. They made us wait outside even though you are a midwife. Other people said they heard bells while they worked. But Tamsin and her baby lived, with nothing worse than marks on James' head. Why are you so angry now, so much later?"

"Indeed. Remember that some of the midwives we spoke to said some of the mothers said it felt like he inserted something metal into them? And those markings, one on each side James' head? Those appear on most all babies Peter Chamberlen delivers this way, and everyone including *that man* agreed that was normal when they delivered a babe this way."

This was not clarifying a thing for her mother.

Eyes slits, hands clenched so hard her nails drew blood, Alice took a deep breath before unclenching (slightly) and continuing. "This delivery I just saw, with the forceps. When they removed the child, it had the same marks."

Thomasine understood immediately and gasped. "They have had this simple tool and kept it from all others so they can make more money!"

Alice ground out her words. "Just so, mother. The greedy bastard let women and infants die when midwives everywhere could have been using this tool. They helped a few women of means in London while women without means died or lost their child, and women in all other areas, with or without means, died or lost their child. So they could keep a monopoly on a simple tool that saves lives."

Thomasine dropped onto a chair, shocked to her core that those men were so willing to let women and children die. "We must all make a living and they should profit from their work, but to keep what they found secret? When it could save so many lives? That is too much." Thomasine crossed herself, thinking of all the deaths caused by their greed.

After ten or fifteen minutes, Alice's fury calmed, as did her mother's. "Truly, mother, God has guided us here. The Americans could not know of Peter Chamberlen, and no one in England would connect their miraculous machine with such a small and simple tool, if they even heard of it, not for a long time, at least. Now that we have, it is a simple matter to send a few of these 'forceps' to the right people in England, people who will publicize it, make others aware that it is what that Chamberlen man has used with such success, and find smiths to make more of them." Her smile was a very thin, cold thing. "Very soon, Peter Chamberlen will find his business much diminished, the profits nearly gone, and women will find their childbirth does not risk putting them in the poorhouse just because they need a simple tool."

Her smile could have frozen the Thames, even on an August day like this.

September 1633

Alice stopped by Kudzu Werke. "Do you have the plans and sample forceps ready yet, Master Glauber?"

"Just. Jakob Betche did most of the work. The forceps were, of course, the easy part, being such a simple tool, and much requested. Making them is good practice for our more advanced apprentices. You should know that the only reason we took on something this simple is because we wish to have the opportunity to manufacture more medical equipment. We spend most of our time making items that require a great deal more precision. Writing the instructions in English was much more challenging, but we persevered. Our final step was finding a smith who had never seen forceps and having him make a set, working from our directions. The one we found made a few suggestions for clarifying points. And now," Herman stopped, looking more closely at Alice. "Are you alright?"

Alice's pain was written clearly across not just her face but her entire rigid body. As it ebbed, she sank into the closest chair. Her answering smile was somewhat uncertain. "Indeed, I am most healthy, I am simply about to have a child. Quite possibly within a few hours, most certainly within the day. But I wish to finish this business first, so please continue."

Herman Glauber looked dubious, but picked up where he had left off. "Both English and German language instructions are complete, and we have several forceps for you. There are variations in the design based on personal and stylistic preferences of the apprentices, but we suspect that midwives may similarly have preferences in things like the shape of the handles. While you are welcome to examine them, it is our recommendation that no decision be made until they have been field-tested, which I understand is being planned. With that, our business here is done and one of our apprentices will see you to Leahy."

Alice was fully aware of how far she had pushed her luck, but equally certain she didn't want to have her baby in this "hospital" instead of at home, as was proper, so she had been trying to hide her contractions all day. Unfortunately for her, Herr Glauber recognized what was happening, and how close her contractions were becoming. Seeing that her contraction was ending and she was about to argue, he called Jakob over. "Please take Frau Blower to Leahy immediately, making sure she doesn't stop anywhere along the way. I will call the hospital to let them know she is on the way and at the rate things seem to be moving, she may deliver in the entryway if they aren't prepared to move her straight to a birthing room. Mrs. Blower, do not get this young man in trouble by not doing as I have said. Now, both of you, go!"

Jakob and Alice went. Twenty minutes later, five minutes after her husband arrived, Alice was holding her newest daughter. Thomas looked at them both, then laughed. "I'll give you credit, Alice, you almost avoided having a hospital delivery!"

She smiled back, "I did my best, husband, I certainly did my best, but Herr Glauber and young Jakob made sure I got here before the birth, so I have now experienced a hospital birth. They tell me I must stay here for three days, for some reason, so you will be watching all the other children for three days."

"Ah, no. I will not. Why should I be doing extra work while you have a bit of a hospital holiday? That's why we have your mother living with us, is it not?"

"A hospital holiday, is it? When I've just pushed a human being out of myself after spending nine whole months making the little one?" Their banter continued as her gurney was pushed down the hall into her room. As the orderly and a nurse started to leave, Alice panicked. "No! This is not my room! We cannot afford for me to have my own room! Please! Even a ward is expensive for us! I cannot stay here!"

The nurse came back to her, gently pushing her back into her bed. "Mrs. Blower, we understand, truly, but we were given instructions when you joined the staff. You are helping to design our training programs, and you are the *only* one designing them who can experience it as a patient. We need to know what we are doing well and if we need to change anything. There will be no charge for your stay, but we are to treat you as we would a patient recovering from a c-section, regardless of whether you have one. And that is exactly what we are going to do, with the only exception being that you can go home after three days with no follow-up scheduled until one-month post-partum. If you argue, all you will do is upset the staff, so please accept this. Also, we aren't quite there yet, but this *is* the plan for our standard room. It is a shared room, not a private room, although we will have those on a more limited basis. Wards are too noisy and patients can make each other sick too easily."

Reluctantly, Alice leaned back and nodded. "I need a notebook and pen to keep notes." Relieved when the nurse nodded and left to get the needed supplies, Alice turned to her grinning husband.

Amused, Thomas watched Alice settle herself and their new baby. "A hospital holiday, like I said. They will be making your food, cleaning the dishes, all manner of things you would never dream of having someone else do at home." Thomas leaned over to kiss her forehead and smooth back her hair. "And you deserve it. Your mother and I will be fine with the other children. You enjoy resting here with our new bairn."

Alice swatted him, then took his hand in hers as she tried, unsuccessfully, to hide a rather large yawn. "You stop hanging out with those Scotsmen!" She handed their new daughter to Thomas. "Now, it is time for me to nap while you hold your baby daughter." With that, Alice squeezed his hand, then pulled the bedding up to her nose to hide her grin as he got a pungent whiff from their new daughter's diaper.

Author's Note:

Alice Blower and her family are historical characters. She was born Alice Frost, daughter of Thomasine Frost, and was a skilled midwife. She emigrated to Boston with her husband, Thomas Blower, and their children in 1635. He died a few years later and she remarried, becoming Alice Tilly. In America, she was brought up on charges as a midwife and jailed. The details of those charges have been lost to time. Alice's arrest caused what is considered the first women's political movement in America. Women wrote, petitioned, and generally fought against what was being done to Alice Tilly. They succeeded in getting permission for her to leave jail in order to deliver babies and perform her job as a midwife.

Historical information on these people puts some hard guardrails around how I can portray them. Alice was apparently not very nice to mothers who were laboring, but she was very, *very* good as a midwife. Good enough that people noted in correspondence that she was not nice but still demanded her release from jail to do her job. As a result, I can't make her soft and kind to laboring mothers.

Susanna was one of the key complainants against Alice in Boston. There isn't any information on possible previous interactions between them, and the ones given in this story certainly didn't happen, but I used this alternate world to add background that would explain the depth of her anger toward Alice.

Martha Haffield is also a historical person. She was noted as abusive and neglectful of her step-children, which I have included in this story. Finally, Peter Chamberlen, his family, and their discovery and use of forceps are also historical, as is the fact that they hid their discovery from others.

State Library Papers

Non Fiction

The North Atlantic Net

Jack Carroll

The original 1632 novel confronted our fictional friends with the Maunder Minimum, a unique period in early modern times when solar activity stayed abnormally low for decades. Ionospheric skip in the high frequency bands, between 3.5 and 30 megahertz (MHz), is how hams traditionally accomplish long-distance communication at modest power levels, with antennas that a private individual can put up. Skip was elusive by the 1630s, if it was there at all. Perhaps the situation wasn't quite as difficult in actual history as it's portrayed in 1632 canon, but there was nobody using radio then to leave us historical records.

With the equipment, the antennas, and the technical knowledge the eighteen original hams in Grantville had immediately to hand, anything much beyond twenty miles or so was severely limited by short daily openings in the lowest ham bands, covering limited spans of longitude. Rick Boatright's "Radio in the 1632 Universe" series, beginning in the first Grantville Gazette and available on the 1632 authors' web site (), explains those problems in detail, and what the hams were able to do about it. My article, "Marine Radio in the 1632 Universe" (*Grantville Gazette* 52), goes into much more detail.

Nevertheless, after vacuum tubes came into production in 1635, there's a rush by governments and large businesses in several countries to establish long-distance communication, especially across salt water. There is even a commercial radiotelegraph route across the North Atlantic (*1637: The Coast of Chaos*). The North Atlantic net that logically grows out from this backbone service has two major functions: commercial radiotelegrams and assistance to ships traveling the North Atlantic sailing route.

How is this possible under such conditions, within a realistic depiction of real-world radio, and the means our fictional characters have at their disposal?

It comes down to the realities of radio propagation—the interaction between the electromagnetic wave and the physical properties of the sea and the atmosphere, propagation loss, natural background noise, transmitter power, and antenna gain and directionality. In other words, it's complicated, but with the right reference material it can be calculated with fair accuracy. Our down-time friends don't have all the published reference material we do, so they will have to rediscover it partly by accident and partly by patient measurements ("Proposal and Counterproposal," *Grantville Gazette* 91).

Frequency is key here. Historical experience with marine radio in the twentieth century is that lower frequencies, from the bottom of the AM broadcast band on down, behave far differently during periods of low solar activity than the high frequencies that hams know. The transition seems to be in the neighborhood of 700 kilohertz (KHz). In these lower bands, useful ionospheric skip is available after dark, usually for several hours, even when the sun is at one of its periodic 11-year minimums. And that is why there is a ship band centered on 500 KHz. This band also works well at any time for ground-wave propagation across the surface of the sea, but in this article we're concerned with its much longer reach by way of night-time skip.

1637: The Coast of Chaos, Chapter 8, says "There were two big radios in their gear, one for the directional transatlantic communication between New Amsterdam and Amsterdam, and hence into the radio communications network that tied the Low Countries together and connected them to the USE." If interpreted literally, that would be a single transatlantic path of 5853 km, which seems overly ambitious, even in these northern latitudes. But if it's interpreted as a short-haul domestic link from Amsterdam to the big shore station at Vlissingen, followed by way of a relay through the major Danish station at Cape Race, Newfoundland, we have one over-water leg of 4057 km and a second of 1793 km. That's much more practical, considering that path loss is approximately an exponential function of distance multiplied by a modified inverse square law, not a linear relationship. Beyond a certain point, the power requirement and antenna size reach absurd levels with startling suddenness. That's just how the math works.

The ship bringing this radio gear sails from Europe in September 1636. The date is important. It's about 8 months after the completion of the designs for a complete suite of tubes for a high-power transmitter and a purpose-built communications receiver. It just fits within the projected vacuum tube timeline, which other stories have been following.

In the propagation and signal-to-noise ratio calculations that follow, we'll turn to night-time sky wave at 500 KHz and 150 KHz. While sky wave is highly variable, extensive data in *Naval Shore Electronics Criteria: VLF, LF, and MF Communication Systems* and in a BBC report on propagation at 150 KHz gives us reasonable confidence that even the quiet-sun ionosphere would support skip on these lower bands starting a couple hours after sunset. Anecdotally, the "NMO Report," reminiscing on the experiences of operating at the old Coast Guard station in Honolulu, says that the whole Pacific typically opened up on 500 KHz around 9 PM every night. That station operated for decades, through many sunspot cycles.

With medium or low frequency sky wave, reliable night-time transoceanic communication at high latitudes would be possible at manageable power levels. While these bands call for transmitting antennas far too large to fit in a ham's back yard—hence, the up-time hams have little or no experience with them—an antenna for some of these lower frequencies and the land to build it on are affordable for a national government or a well-capitalized commercial radio communication enterprise.

Calculations are shown for several bands, to explore what is possible. While several of the longer paths offer lower power requirements at 250 KHz or less, the towers they would require are probably not affordable in the 1630s. A standard quarter-wave vertical for 500 KHz is 150 meters tall, and that's probably about the practical limit for wood lattice construction. The steel industry is still struggling to meet domestic demand during this period. Also, although suitable timber can be found near many of the station sites, steel would have to be shipped across the ocean. So, while steel towers for 200 or 250 KHz are possible in principle, they aren't practical at this time. Anything below 250 KHz based on wooden towers would require two of them, not one, to support a T-antenna with horizontal loading wires across the top. (Not only that, a T antenna loses 3 decibels (dB) at the preferred low radiation angle because of its less optimum vertical radiation pattern. That would require doubling the transmitter power to compensate.)

So, the 500 KHz band becomes the practical compromise choice.

Published data shows a nightly opening lasting up to 8 hours. A single sky wave hop covers up to 2000 km; longer distances require multiple hops.

When the intermediate ground reflection is off sea water, the losses are low enough to support paths of two or three hops in these bands.

Signals, noise, and bandwidth

Here we omit a long section from the earlier article, explaining the details of the relationship between the natural atmospheric noise level at each receiving site and the power needed at the distant transmitting station, in order to achieve an adequate signal-to-noise ratio so that the radio operator can copy an incoming message at a commercial speed of 25 words per minute. That material is fully explained in the earlier article, "Marine Radio in the 1632 Universe" (*Grantville Gazette* 52). We merely summarize with a list of the peak noise levels to be expected at the station sites desired in the North Atlantic net, within the narrowest bandwidth suitable for copying at full commercial speed.

Location	30 KHz	150 KHz	500 KHz	2 MHz	4 MHz
North Germany, Netherlands, Southern Scandinavia, Ingria 50°–60°N, 0°–30°E {nom. +70}	-11 dBm	-42 dBm	-69 dBm	-87 dBm	-94 dBm
Cape Clear 51°N, 10°W {nom. +60}	-18 dBm	-52 dBm	-79 dBm	-97 dBm	-103 dBm
New Amsterdam 40°N, 73°W {nom. +85}	-6 dBm	-32 dBm	-52 dBm	-70 dBm	-78 dBm
Suriname, West Indies 6°N, 55°W {nom. +85}	-6 dBm	-32 dBm	-52 dBm	-70 dBm	-78 dBm
Tampa 28°N, 82°W {nom. +85}	-6 dBm	-32 dBm	-52 dBm	-70 dBm	-78 dBm
Cape Race 47°N, 53°W {nom. +67}	-12 dBm	-48 dBm	-71 dBm	-90 dBm	-98 dBm
Bermuda 32°N, 65°W {nom. +82}	-9 dBm	-35 dBm	-55 dBm	-73 dBm	-81 dBm
St. Eustatius 17°N, 63°W (nom. +85)	-6 dBm	-32 dBm	-52 dBm	-70 dBm	78 dBm

Required signal-to-noise ratio

The *Radio Propagation Handbook* contains a table of recommended signal-to-noise ratios relative to the noise in a 1 Hz bandwidth, for different grades of service with several types of modulation used in commercial service. We'll confine our analysis to Morse code, because that requires much less bandwidth than any form of voice communication, and so demands much less transmitter power than any alternative available in the first decades of the NTL. For hand-sent Morse code the handbook gives +36 dB relative to the noise in a 1 Hz bandwidth for "operator-to-operator" service. But commercial Morse code implies a typical receiver bandwidth of roughly 100 Hz to handle a 25 WPM keying rate, not 1 Hz, so the noise power passing through the filter is 100 times greater, or 20 dB stronger. Hence, the signal-to-noise ratio in the actual bandwidth needed to achieve that grade of service is +16 dB. A good operator could copy through a somewhat worse signal-to-noise ratio, but it would be tiring and probably result in errors and dropouts.

The same table recommends +45 dB above the noise in a 1 Hz bandwidth for "good commercial service," which would be +25 dB above our calculated levels.

We'll use +16 dB as the criterion for our basic power / path loss / antenna gain calculations.

In the following table, P_{signal} assumes a transmitter power of 1 KW. The transmitting antenna at 500 KHz is assumed to be a full-size quarter wave vertical on a good ground plane. For the lower bands a shortened vertical is assumed, which typically delivers a 3 dB weaker signal at the low takeoff angles desired for skip or ground wave. The path loss numbers for 500 KHz are extrapolated, and so less certain.

Baseline case: non-directional receiving antennas

Baseline case: non-directional receiving antennas

Path	Value, Units	100 KHz SKY	150 KHz SKY	200 KHz SKY	500 KHz SKY
Cape Clear to Cape Race, 3181 km, 2 hops	A_{path}, dB	-80	-90?	-100	-120?
	P_{signal}, dBm	-20	-30?	-40	-57?
	P_{noise}, dBm	-35	-44	-51	-81
	S/N, dB	+15	+14?	+11	+24?
	P_{16dB}, W	1.2K	1.6K?	3.2K	160?
Cape Race to Vlissingen, 4057 km, 2 hops (Eastbound is the more unfavorable direction. The North Sea coast is about 2 dB noisier than Newfoundland.)	A_{path}, dB	-83	-94?	-105	-127?
	P_{signal}, dBm	-23	-34?	-45	-67?
	P_{noise}, dBm	-31	-42	-44	-69
	S/N, dB	+8	+8	+1	+2
	P_{16dB}, W	6.3K	6.3K	32K	25K
Cape Race to New Amsterdam, 1793 km, 1 hop	A_{path}, dB	-76	-77?	-78	-79?
	P_{signal}, dBm	16	-17?	-18	19?
	P_{noise}, dBm	-36	-45	-52	-82
	S/N, dB	+20	+28	+34	+63
	P_{16dB}, W	400	63	16	2

Cape Race to Bermuda, 1882 km, 1 hop	A_{path}, dB	-76	-77?	-78	-79?
	P_{signal}, dBm	-16	-17?	-18	-19?
	P_{noise}, dBm	-22	-35	-36	-55
	S/N, dB	+6	+18	+18	+36
	P_{16dB}, W	10K	200	200	10
Bermuda to St. Eustatius, 1657 km, 1 hop	A_{path}, dB	-66	-71?	-77	-78?
	P_{signal}, dBm	-6	-11?	-17	-18?
	P_{noise}, dBm	-25	-32	-39	-52
	S/N, dB	+19	+21	+22	+34
	P_{16dB}, W	500	316	250	180

Bermuda to Suriname, 3277 km, 2 hops	A_{path}, dB	-80	-90?	-99	-110?
	P_{signal}, dBm	-20	-30?	-39	-50?
	P_{noise}, dBm	-25	-32	-39	-52
	S/N, dB	+5	+2	0	+2
	P_{16dB}, W	8K	25K	40K	25K
Amsterdam to New Amsterdam, 5853 km, 3 hops	A_{path}, dB	-96	-110?	-123	-150?
	P_{signal}, dBm	-36	-50?	-63	-90?
	P_{noise}, dBm	-31	-42	-44	-69
	S/N, dB	-5	-8	-19	-21
	P_{16dB}, W	126K	250K	3.2M	5M
St. Eustatius to Suriname, 1544 km, 1 hop	A_{path}, dB	-66	-71?	-77	-78?
	P_{signal}, dBm	-6	-11?	-17	-18
	P_{noise}, dBm	-25	-32	-39	-52
	S/N, dB	+19	+21	+22	+34
	P_{16dB}, W	500	316	251	16

Improving the situation

Clearly, some of these paths sorely need a little help from the receiving antenna. Twentieth-century coastal stations tended to have large collections of directional receiving antennas, such as rhombics and Beverage arrays. The benefit of a directional receiving antenna is that the only noise it accepts is what arrives from its sensitive direction, where the signal is coming from. It rejects noise coming from any other direction. The narrower the main lobe, the less noise it picks up.

The size and complexity of the antenna can be traded off against the narrowness of its sensitive main lobe—its directionality. It's important to note that in the medium- and low-frequency ranges, the atmospheric noise is orders of magnitude stronger than the receiver's internal noise. Thus, it's acceptable for the receiving antenna to be wildly lossy, as long as it's directional.

The classic directional receiving antenna for medium down to very low-frequency bands is the Beverage wave antenna, developed in the early 1920s. It consists of a horizontal wire supported on a line of poles, running above the earth from the receiver toward the incoming signal, for a distance of 1/2 to 2 wavelengths. It needs to be only high enough to clear people and vehicles passing underneath, and according to Dr. Beverage's notes, the earth underneath is a functional part of the antenna—and the cause of its lossiness. It behaves electrically as a leaky transmission line, magnetically coupled to the traveling wave. It receives in both endwise directions. Noise arriving from the undesired direction would reflect off the far end of the line and come back toward the receiver, except that the far end of the line is terminated with a resistor to absorb that unwanted power and dissipate it as heat. Dr. Beverage's experiments found, and later mathematical analysis confirmed, that performance doesn't improve at lengths greater than 2 wavelengths, due to the difference in wave propagation speed on the line versus wave speed in free space.

Published papers I've found don't give numerical values for the improvement in received signal-to-noise ratio with this type of antenna. One ham reports an improvement over an omnidirectional antenna of +11 dB. Dr. Beverage built arrays of as many as four elements across, spaced far enough apart so as not to overlap their apertures, and phase-combined at the receiver, giving an additional improvement of up to +6 dB over a single wave antenna element. So, we can estimate a possible improvement of +17 dB over an omnidirectional receiving antenna at a large commercial receiving site.

The attractive thing about a wave antenna is that it doesn't involve tall towers or other large structures. Even at 150 KHz, it would be no more than 4 kilometers long. A single Beverage antenna could be installed at any coastal station outside a built-up area at a very early date.

There are other directional wire antennas for these frequency bands, but hams have practical literature and some experience with the Beverage. I saw one in use at the Nashua Amateur Radio Society's Field Day site in 2022. In other words, this type of antenna is known in Grantville.

Improved case: directional receiving antennas

In the following table, the effect on required transmitter power is calculated for four different receiving antenna configurations.

Omni is a non-directional antenna, such as the station's transmitting tower or a small shortened non-resonant version. The power required to achieve a +16 dB S/N in a 100 Hz bandwidth with this configuration is carried down from the previous table. The power required by each of the improved receiving antenna arrays follows on successive lines.

Single is a single Beverage wave antenna. Signal-to-noise ratio improvement factor: +11 dB.

Dual is a pair of Beverage antennas in parallel, spaced far enough apart so that their capture apertures don't overlap. S/N improvement factor: +14 dB.

Quad is a set of four Beverage antennas in parallel. S/N improvement factor: +17 dB.

Path	Antenna	100 KHz P_{16dB}, W	150 KHz P_{16dB}, W	200 KHz P_{16dB}, W	500 KHz P_{16dB}, W
Cape Clear to Cape Race, 3181 km, 2 hops	Omni	1.2K	1.6K?	3.2K	160?
	Single	95	127	254	12.7
	Dual	48	64	127	6.4
	Quad	24	32	64	3.2
Cape Race to Vlissingen, 4057 km, 2 hops (Eastbound is the more unfavorable direction. The North Sea coast is about 2 dB noisier than Newfoundland.)	Omni	6.3K	6.3K	32K	25K
	Single	500	500	2.54K	2K
	Dual	250	250	1.27K	1K
	Quad	125	125	640	500
Cape Race to New Amsterdam, 1793 km, 1 hop	Omni	400	63	16	2
	Single	32	5	1.27	0.16
	Dual	16	2.5	0.64	0.08
	Quad	8	1.3	1.32	0.04
Cape Race to Bermuda, 1882 km, 1 hop	Omni	10K	200	200	10
	Single	794	16	16	0.794
	Dual	397	8	8	0.397
	Quad	199	4	4	0.199
Bermuda to St. Eustatius, 1657 km, 1 hop	Omni	500	316	250	158
	Single	39.7	25.1	19.9	12.6
	Dual	19.9	12.6	9.93	6.3
	Quad	9.93	6.3	4.96	3.1

Bermuda to Suriname, 3277 km, 2 hops	Omni	8K	25K	40K	25K
	Single	635	1.99K	3.2K	1.99K
	Dual	318	993	1.6K	993
	Quad	159	496	800	496
Amsterdam to New Amsterdam, 5853 km, 3 hops	Omni	126K	250K	3.2M	5M
	Single	10K	19.9K	254K	397K
	Dual	5K	9.93K	127K	199K
	Quad	2.5K	4.96K	64K	99K

Path	Value, Units	100 KHz SKY	150 KHz SKY	200 KHz SKY	500 KHz SKY
Cape Race to Suriname, 4530 km, 2 hops	Omni	1.6K	3.2K?	5K	12.6K?
	Single	127	254	3.97K	1K
	Dual	64	127	1.99K	500
	Quad	32	64	9.9K	250

Further improved case: directional receiving antennas along with directional transmitting antennas

Directional receiving antennas reduce most of these cases to fairly reasonable power requirements. This is not the case of direct communication between Amsterdam and New Amsterdam, though. The three-hop path is just a hop too far. The USE navy's barely usable link between Vlissingen and St. Eustatius was based on an omnidirectional transmitting antenna at Vlissingen, and required a 40-kilowatt alternator transmitter to occasionally be heard through the atmospheric noise at the Caribbean tropical latitude, during moments when the noise dropped. Getting a 25-word message through was expected to take a week of repetitions, night after night.

This is far from acceptable for a commercial service. As we see above, for the three-hop route to New Amsterdam, the numbers show a required transmitting power with an omnidirectional receiving antenna of 5 megawatts, and with a four-bay Beverage receiving antenna, 99 kilowatts, more than twice the output of the big navy transmitter. Something more is needed.

The single-tower Vlissingen transmitting antenna was canonized in *1636: Commander Cantrell in the West Indies*. The New Netherlands action in *1637: The Coast of Chaos* is set later, mostly in 1637. We could plausibly add a dedicated directional transmitting antenna for that story line, built later and consisting of a wire Yagi suspended between two towers. That wouldn't be inordinately expensive; it would cost around 2.5 times as much as a single-tower omnidirectional antenna. One reference gives these more-or-less typical gain figures for common Yagi configurations:

Approximate Yagi-Uda antenna gain levels

Number of elements	Approx anticipated gain dB over dipole
2	5
3	7.5
4	8.5
5	9.5
6	10.5
7	11.5

Let's say the Amsterdam end transmits with a six to eight element Yagi and New Amsterdam receives with a four-bay Beverage. That increases the power density in the main beam by a factor of at least 14.1 and reduces the power needed to achieve a +16 dB worst-case S/N to 7 kilowatts. That's a lot for a tube transmitter in the 1637 time frame, but not totally unreasonable. Otherwise, it might be an alternator transmitter, falling between the 3.2 kilowatt unit on St. Eustatius and the 40 kilowatt monster at Vlissingen.

Obviously, it would be a lot cheaper to relay through Cape Race, but maybe the Dutch government considers it politically risky to rely on a

Danish relay station. If they're willing to spend big guilders to put up big arrays at both ends of the path in both directions, they can bring the whole service in house. In any case, the service is in canon, with a transmitting tube in New Amsterdam a foot in diameter. That could generate something in the neighborhood of 10 kilowatts. (Finding a source of flowing water capable of generating that much electricity close to the city could be an interesting problem.)

Economics and practical station designs

The numbers shown here represent the minimum transmitter power required for specified conditions. That doesn't mean the designers and managers of these stations will literally select those power levels.

The standard reference publications choose 1 kilowatt for a reason. That's a typical commercial power level for a ship or a shore station communicating on these bands. In "Proposal and Counterproposal" (*Grantville Gazette* 91), Miller guesses that a kilowatt will be about the amount of power required to meet the Venetians' objectives. It turns out he's right.

From a transmitter design viewpoint, 1 kilowatt is about right for a "standard" 500 KHz ship transmitter. It gives good range using saltwater ground-wave propagation in the daytime, and skip at night. It's not excessively expensive or bulky, and its electrical input requirement of 1.5 to 2 kilowatts is within reason for a small shipboard generator. These transmitters are usually able to operate at reduced power levels, to minimize interference to other stations when full power is not needed.

The availability of these rigs makes them attractive for shore stations as well. They don't have to be specially ordered, and they would be available with the first generation of power tubes.

On the other hand, would most of the point-to-point links actually be designed for the minimum acceptable signal quality of +16 dB in a 100 Hz bandwidth? Probably not. It's less tiring to copy at +25 dB. Further, the operators would rather use a receiving filter width of 200 to 500 Hz. The signal doesn't ring as much that way. It would make a lot of sense to aim for +6 to +10 dB stronger received signals, as long as it isn't too expensive in transmitter power and receiving antenna complexity—bearing in mind that one of these major stations would require a receiver and antenna pointed at each of the other sites (or shipping lanes) where quality service is desired. In some cases two or more partner stations might be close enough in azimuth to fall within the main lobe of a single antenna, but that wouldn't always be the case.

An interesting aspect of the economics is how radiotelegram services would be paid for in a net where every station has a different owner of a different nationality. There could be a story in that.

Follow-on developments

In this article we've concentrated on the essential backbone stations needed to form a useful North Atlantic radiotelegraph net. But the build-out of radio communication in the Americas wouldn't end there. As tube production ramps up and costs come down over the next few years, it will become affordable and attractive to grow local nets, spreading out from each of these long-haul stations. These will look more like up-time ham stations, using high frequencies, small and affordable antennas, and modest power. They will extend the services of the backbone net out to smaller communities at a distance from the major stations. In Europe, the existing postal services based on the long-established road network, and the availability at relatively high cost of carrier pigeon services, reduce the incentive to expand short-haul radio service. But in the North American colonies there are few roads, and almost none between communities. It's all river traffic from the interior to the coast, and sailing coasters from harbor to harbor. And nobody has an organized pigeon service. Radio service from town to town to carry messages and news could look pretty attractive.

Once this kind of equipment is available and affordable, ham radio itself may take root in the New World. Tube gear is a lot more satisfactory for the operator than spark.

But radiotelegraph isn't the end of the story for the transatlantic net. Suppose that after the initial suite of tube designs reaches production, and GE's tube engineering group takes on VHF and UHF as its next priority, the Dutch branch of the consortium decides to concentrate on high power medium frequency tubes? The obvious application is medium frequency AM broadcasting and low frequency single-sideband broadcasting. The technology can also be used to create a transatlantic telephone trunk using single-sideband modulation. That would place a real premium on noise-reducing receiving antennas. And as it happens, that's exactly what Dr. Beverage and his team were working on in 1921.

As demand grows, more new engineering graduates join the work force, and technology matures, some of these links may be upgraded from single-channel to multi-channel, using the same antennas. That, too, was being done in 1921.

If an iron and steel industry starts up in New Jersey, as it very well could over the next few years, that could introduce a wild card into the radio picture. It would become possible to build much taller transmitting antennas without shipping hundreds of tons of material across the ocean. That would open the 150–250 KHz region, with its lower propagation losses, to multi-channel voice service.

In one important sense, the net as described here is incomplete. It gives good service to the east coast colonies, but it's severely limited in its service to shipping. It only covers the homeward part of the sailing route that follows the oceanic wind circulation. There is no coverage of the outward bound route, southward along the west coast of Europe and then westward in the trade winds. All the prospective sites for shore stations—the Azores, the Canaries, Madeira, Portugal, France—are in hostile territory. There has been some muttering that a revolt against the Spanish crown might break out in Portugal within the next few years. And if that happens, the Braganzas might see advantages in developing some type of cordial relationship with the USE, the Dutch, the Kalmar powers, and even Venice. But as we look at European politics in 1637, we can only speculate, and await developments.

In our NTL world, there is no obvious way to further extend the medium frequency skip net beyond the North Atlantic. There are no likely places to establish stations farther south, the noise levels in the equatorial zone are particularly difficult, and the chain of relays becomes unattractively long. That's why GE and GRL are pushing on to VHF and moonbounce. In the next few years that will open up direct radio contact with more than half the world, and single-relay contact with the rest. Moonbounce has its own timing limitations due to orbital mechanics, but it should do until the satellites go up a century hence.

References

American Radio Relay League. *The ARRL Antenna Book*, 13th ed. Newington, CT, 1974.

American Radio Relay League, Radio Society of Great Britain. *VHF/UHF Handbook.* ISBN: 9781-9050-8631-3. Chapter 30, "Space

Communications." http://physics.princeton.edu/pulsar/K1JT/Hbk_2010_Ch30_EME.pdf http://physics.princeton.edu/pulsar/K1JT/EME_2010_Hbk.pdf

Belrose, J.S. et al. "Beverage Antennas for Amateur Communications." QST Magazine, January 1983, p.22. http://nrcdxas.org/articles/Beverage0183.pdf

British Broadcasting Corporation, Research Department. "Low-frequency sky-wave propagation to distances of about 2000 km", Report No. 1971/8. http://downloads.bbc.co.uk/rd/pubs/reports/1971-08.pdf

Boatright, Rick. "Radio FAQ Part 4: RF Environment." https://author.1632magazine.com/technology/radio-faq-part-4-rf-environment/

Department of the Navy, Naval Electronic Systems Command. *Naval Shore Electronics Criteria: VLF, LF, and MF Communication Systems.* Washington: U. S. Government Printing Office, 1972. FSN 0280-901-1000 http://www.navy-radio.com/manuals/0101-1xx/0101_113-00.pdf through -08.pdf

Kraus, John D. *Antennas.* New York: McGraw-Hill, 1950. ISBN 07-035410-3

Maritime Radio Historical Society. "Reports from NMO." http://radiomarine.org/gallery/show?keyword=pt3&panel=pab1_8#pab1_8

Navy Radio web pages. "NAA Cutler Maine - Navy VLF Transmitter Site." http://www.navy-radio.com/commsta/cutler.htm

Payne, Craig. *Principles of Naval Weapon Systems.* Annapolis, MD: Naval Institute Press, 2006. ISBN 1-59114-658-5 books.google.com/books?isbn=1591146585

Saveskie, Peter N. *Radio Propagation Handbook.* Blue Ridge Summit, PA: Tab Books, 1980. ISBN 0-8306-9949-X, ISBN 0-8306-1146-0 paperback.

W8JI. "How Low-noise Receiving Antennas Really Work." http://www.w8ji.com/receiving.htm

https://www.electronics-notes.com/articles/antennas-propagation/yagi-uda-antenna-aerial/gain-directivity.php

Bang Versus Twang In North America

John Deakins

Throughout the seventeenth century, many personal missile weapons were in use. A particular problem with those occurred in North America. A French expedition had conquered the English settlements at Boston and Plymouth. English King Charles I had signed away his New World possessions to the French, in exchange for royal cash. To fight back, the Massachusetts English settlers needed the Native American tribes. French muskets were so superior, however, that the natives needed to be rearmed with better weapons, or the contest would be over.

Meanwhile, in western New York, beyond the border of then-New Netherlands, Eliezer St. Clair, a Pequot adopted as a Mohawk sachem, knew what would happen when white settlements got around to expanding westward. (A Red Son Rises in the West and A Red Son: Not Without Honor; Ring of Fire Press) The Five Nations of the Iroquois, the best organized tribes, stood in their way. St. Clair and his Oneida wife had blunted the smallpox plagues that would have weakened them, introduced ironworking, provided the Iroquois with their own written language, and begun modern agriculture. Nevertheless, the Iroquois would still go under when facing European musketry. They needed better weapons.

Native Americans loved muskets. They traded for them as often as possible, but they still had only a relative handful. The tribes needed quickly produced, competitive weapons until their entire force was properly armed. What was available?

Wheellock Firearms

A spring-loaded wheel spins a serrated edge against iron pyrites, creating a spark to ignite the powder. They were complex weapons, expensive to build and maintain, rich men's weapons. They took about a minute to load, and they tended to misfire about 40% of the time. Why bother?

All muskets were terror weapons to uncivilized natives, thunder sticks which smoked, boomed, and shot sparks of partly burned powder. They had greater range than native bows. They could be held on target longer. The musket might weigh ten to twelve pounds, while the tension that had to be held on a bowstring was measured in the tens of pounds.

A native would be glad to own a wheellock, but it would have broken down in short order.

Matchlock Firearms

The matchlock fires its primer powder with a continually burning slow-match fuse, possibly as simple as rope soaked in ammonia. They were simpler to make, but they, too, had drawbacks. They couldn't be operated in the rain, and the match could accidentally ignite a soldier's powder supply. If the fuse went out, relighting it under battlefield conditions might be impossible. It, too, was slow to load and had a misfire rate of 40%. If a thousand troops fired a volley, only 600 shots actually went off.

Flintlock Firearms

The flintlock came into common usage only two or three decades before the Ring of Fire. A spring-loaded hammer caused a flint to knock a spark into a priming pan. A trained professional could load a musket three times a minute, but even twice a minute was faster than older weapons. They had a 30% misfire rate, so that a thousand-man volley gained 100 shots over a similar unit armed with matchlocks. More accurate, with a longer range, they were becoming common among European nations. French muskets outclassed every native weapon or trade-musket. What happened to the older models? After a battle, no one would want the wheellocks or matchlocks, not with flintlocks sweeping the fields and modern weapons on the way.

My guess would be that farmers all over the Germanies became musketeers, mainly for hunting, armed with the discarded wheellocks and matchlocks. In North America, obsolete muskets would be the first traded to the natives. Inferior metal and broken parts would shorten their service compared to that of prestige weapons. There'd never be enough of them in service to make a difference to scattered North American natives.

Percussion-cap Firearms

Cap-and-ball pistols and percussion-cap rifles raised a volley's efficiency to only 20% misfires or better. We've reached the age of current seventeenth-century technology, pushed by existing American weapons. The European demand was so high that Native Americans would never have seen the more complex system. Percussion caps were hard to make using seventeenth-century manufacturing.

Rifling and Minié Balls

Rifling and Minié balls would quickly be adopted for flintlocks and percussion-locks. They were refinements on an existing pattern. Each spins the bullet and increases accurate range. On the other hand, those would have had little effect in North America. A blacksmith might make a smoothbore musket. A talented smith might add rifling, but those were slow processes. The Iroquois and the Englishmen's native allies needed mass armament, not individual craftsmanship.

Breech-loading and Beyond

Advances were being made across Europe in arming ordinary soldiers with breech-loading rifles. They have five times the rate of fire of a muzzleloader. Flintlock-armed, muzzleloading opponents had to rise to reload, but a breech-loading soldier could remain prone and keep firing. Brass cartridges and automatic weapons faded into the future, with no bearing on the current problem.

Bow and Arrow

What about bows? The bow-and arrow was invented sometime in the Neolithic. They're fast to reload, but they have limited range. Accuracy and penetrating power drop off rapidly at distance. They had battle significance only if a force shot many arrows. Native American accuracy with bows wasn't particularly effective. Many bows could be made rapidly, but the more the process was rushed, the lower the bow quality. Most English refugees had so little experience with bows that arming them would have been pointless.

The English longbow

The English longbow could be argued to be the epitome of bows. A trained archer could shoot three arrows a minute, with pinpoint accuracy at hundreds of yards and beyond. By the seventeenth century, however, their use had dropped off to almost zero. The ideal English longbow required a bow stave of Spanish yew wood, though English yew was acceptable. The bow stave might be six feet (two meters) long. Hand-crafted, hand-straightened arrows ran to three feet (one meter) long. Not only were the weapons difficult to make, but the real problem lay in practice. Hard work was involved. A trained archer needed daily practice. The government held contests and awarded prizes for the best archers. As soon as encouragement from above disappeared, so did the trained archers. English longbows could never be considered a solution to native armament problems.

Mongol bows

The Mongol horsemen used a different solution. Their bows were short and powerful. Each was a laminated, double re-curve bow, ideal for launching many arrows from horseback. Unfortunately, each was also a hand-crafted artifact, made of glued strips of wood and boiled bone. Native Americans would have loved them, but they'd never have had sufficient quantities.

Compound bows

Never mind. The materials are too expensive or require modern technology. The parts are complex. There might be a few in use in Europe, but they'd never reach North America or be produced in quantity.

The crossbow

A bow is mounted on a wooden stock, with a trigger assembly to release the string. They're found worldwide. For example, a Montagnard tribesman in the Vietnam hills could take a knife into the forest and return with a completed crossbow. The bow, quarrels, and stock were traditional wood. The quarrels were fletched with thin bark, and the right kind of vine made the string. Montagnard quarrels have been found lodged in the bodies of American helicopters. Note that no metal, except the original knife, was involved in the manufacture.

European crossbows used steel bow staves. Quarrels were shorter and required less elaborate preparation. An archer mortally wounded Richard the Lionhearted during a castle siege in Germany. The archer was allegedly executed, of course, for regicide. Steel bows and steel strings produce a harder hit than ordinary bows. English longbows and metal crossbows could penetrate chain mail armor.

The steel crossbow, which could be loaded by hand by a strong man, could be made to hit harder and fly farther than a traditional bow. The next generation introduced a long cocking lever, because of the stronger resistance of metal bows, but escalation continued. Within a generation, it required a hand-cranked windlass to pull the string into place. Loading time went from roughly twice a minute to once in five minutes. The crossbow was fine if you were under siege, but it was too slow for many battlefield confrontations. It fell out of use as firearms acquired better reload time, range, and reliability.

The North American problem remains. Two solutions emerged. Kevin and Karen Evans had suggested that a simplified pump shotgun would work. They're smooth-bores, and even an amateur blacksmith could produce one rapidly. It required no elaborate lock, with parts to wear out or break. It could be fired by a pump or slamfire action, similar to that of reloading a pump shotgun's shell. Instead of chambering another round, the action fired a paper cartridge or tamped powder. It was simple to make and to operate. Within months, the refugee English and their native allies could be rearmed.

Eliezer St. Clair had another problem. Native Americans didn't yet work in iron. They understood gold, silver, copper, and lead, but not iron. On the other hand, there were many iron-ore outcroppings inside Mohawk hunting grounds. The potential was there, but the Iroquois had to be trained to burn charcoal and to create crude iron blooms. Then, the iron had to be worked into steel to make crossbow staves. Stocks could be almost any wood, and trigger parts could be whittled from hardwoods.

Steel-wire strings were a future development, but good bowstrings could be manufactured from various sources, including hemp thread. Sinews from deer could be combined with leather. The cleaned and dried intestines of mountain lions, lynxes, and wildcats make excellent bowstrings, but the supply would be limited.

Crossbows were within reach of the Iroquois, but steel could also make hoes, axes, tomahawks, shovels, arrowheads, cooking pots, and (eventually) plows. The more Mohawks were trained to work iron, the more likely each might manufacture his own crossbow. Production would ramp up.

What are the advantages and disadvantages? Both pump guns and crossbows could be held on target far longer than any bow. Both could be produced quickly. Initially, pump guns would probably be more available. Both could be as rapidly fired as a flintlock. Both were much quicker to reload than a matchlock, wheellock, or a rifled musket. Both had significant knock-down power. With many available, the rapidly produced weapons could raise the natives and the refugees to the firepower of the French troops' limited number.

Which Way To Go?

The English would be more comfortable with a gun that went boom! and fired a slug or shot. Lead projectiles might become scarce, but crude shotguns could fire wooden slugs or stone pebbles, if need be. The choke point was gunpowder. Theoretically, an ordinary soldier could make his own gunpowder with sulfur, charcoal, and saltpeter. Charcoal and saltpeter were within the reach of many individuals. In non-volcanic New England, sulfur was uncommon. It had to be imported. The English refugees would soon own guns that they couldn't load. Paper cartridges would only make that worse.

The firing technique also limited the range and accuracy. The pump guns could become the equivalent of the trench broom shotguns of World War I. Up close, they'd be deadly, fast to load, and able to deliver a deadly load. An aimed shot was another matter. The very pumping action that fired them would work at close quarters, but it would disrupt aim at distance. They'd almost certainly be less accurate than a smoothbore musket.

Prediction: The English refugees would initially maul the French troops, but they'd run out of gunpowder. They might steal from the French or trade for expensive New Amsterdam gunpowder, but there were no gunpowder sources in New England itself. Up-close raiders would shock the regulars, until the French fixed bayonets. Trained troops would quickly level the field against opponents already small in numbers. North American successes would accumulate at first, but then drop off without gunpowder.

Meanwhile, it would take years for the Iroquois to universally arm themselves with steel crossbows. However, every tribe had bow makers. They knew local wood. The best bow wood was the bois d'arc, the Osage orange. Unfortunately, that grew no closer than Arkansas or Oklahoma. Some eastern bow makers would travel hundreds of miles to obtain a supply. There are other woods, and the Iroquois bow makers would know them. The potential for mass-produced, all-wooden crossbows existed.

Wood doesn't have the tensile strength of steel, nor does it have the knock-down power of a lead slug. Pump guns could fire shot, wooden bullets, and stone balls. Crossbows had to use arrows. Shorter quarrels, requiring less preparation, would work with steel crossbows, but normal, all-wooden crossbows, with enough penetrating power to be credible, couldn't launch a short quarrel hard enough for anything but small game. The solution is to make the crossbow's wooden bow stave wider and the stock longer, to handle the longer string. Arrows had to be correspondingly longer and straighter. They'd also be harder to make.

The bigger crossbows would collide with the law of diminishing returns. Native Americans were noted for their stealth. They couldn't sustain an English longbow on a wooden stock, while slipping down narrow forest trails, nor struggling with a heavy, awkward, weapons-grade crossbow. Perhaps the wooden crossbows could be carried disassembled, but that would require another level of invention that might not be reached in time. Light native scouts would become heavy infantry, loaded down with a heavy stock, a long bow stave, extra strings, long arrows, steel tomahawk, supplies, and medicine bundle. Inevitably, some workers would develop impossibly big crossbows and have to start over.

As time passed, every Iroquoian would have a wooden crossbow for small game. A steel bow or a large wooden bow could take down deer or bear or be used in war. They could be aimed and held on target. A large bow has the same range and weight as a smoothbore musket. They don't go boom! to frighten the game or to give away the warrior's position to an enemy with powder smoke. They spew no sparks to signal an ambush location in dim light. At most, each makes a thump! a European might recognize. On the other hand, rearming and crossbow development would take months or years.

Projection

The French incursion would be met by the English refugees and their native allies with successful guerrilla raids. In the long run, however, the French would succeed. They were more likely to be stopped by European political developments than by the locals. (See 1636: The French Correction.) The French New England takeover was by a fleet sent by King Gaston. The French colony on the St Lawrence is not necessarily in his camp; it might support his opponent. If Gaston continued to maintain the French presence in Massachusetts, the English rebels would eventually lose.

Relocation to the rugged terrain between Boston and the Lake Champlain/Lake George area could halt French expansion. Dutch influence generally ceased at Albany/Fort Orange, at the Mohawk River junction. Northwest from there belonged to the Five Nations, but up the river to the northeast, the English Puritan refugees could establish a colony. That would work only as long as they remained on good terms with the Algonquian-speaking tribes east of the Hudson. Some of those tribes, foreseeing a French victory, would have changed sides. Guerrilla raids against the French would never have ceased, but the poorly armed English proto-colony could survive in isolation, if they could keep their trigger-happy members from starting an Indian war.

Across the river, the Mohawks had a long history of war with the Algonquian-speakers. They would probably leave the English alone, as long as they stayed east of the river. Influential Eliezer St. Clair was pro-English and anti-French. Speaking Mohegan-Pequot (an Algonquian language), Mohawk-Oneida (an Iroquoian language), and English, he could probably build a negotiated peace.

Looming ahead, there'd be a battle between European-trained troops (probably Gaston-French) and crossbow-armed Iroquois. European expansion westward would run into smallpox-immune, militarily adept natives. The North American future, spawned by the Grantville-trained Eliezer St. Clair, could look quite different.

AVAILABLE NOW

Mrs. Flannery's Flowers

Bethanne Kim

Mrs. Flannery's Flowers

Bethanne Kim

Big things are happening in Grantville since it was sent through time and space to war-torn seventeenth-century Germany, and up-timer nursing student Krystal Reed isn't handling it very well. She never wanted to live in Grantville and being sent back to the seventeenth century just makes it worse. Working with doctors who think bleeding is a legitimate medical practice and that women have no business in medicine is exasperating, to say the least—but their prejudices are no match for the new medical programs in Grantville and Jena. Now if only she can recover from losing her parents, her friends, her home, her college, and her future.

Nils Jorgensen and family are just a few of the thousands of down-timers looking for a new future in Grantville. They arrive with little more than their skills. Through hard work, the Jorgensens start a fashion empire.

For the elderly Irene Flannery, life is more about smaller, personal issues. With no family left up-time, her biggest worry now that she's in the seventeenth century is having a married curate at the Catholic church. (The scandal!) But she has kept a secret since FDR was President and she'll defend her rose bushes to the death because of it.

https://www.baen.com/mrs-flannery-s-flowers.html

Gourmets of Grantville

Bethanne Kim

Gourmets Of Grantville

Bethanne Kim

After traveling through time and space from 2000 in West Virginia to 1631 in Germany, the Grantvillers have to find enough food, medicine, and other supplies to stay alive and healthy while helping their new German neighbors and a constant flow of refugees do the same. Working together, they grow and gather enough food for everyone, but it's not quite what anyone is used to eating. Down-time Germans view potatoes as animal food, unfit for human consumption—until they try their first potato chips. Seeing everyone, including small children, drinking beer instead of water is a big change for the up-timers, just as big a change as seeing people casually drink water and not get sick is for down-timers. But the Grantville Cooking Club proves food is also a bridge, helping up-timers and down-timers work together to create a new cuisine. They also jump-start several new restaurants and businesses.

Meanwhile, regular life continues. How do you keep going when you know that your child, or spouse, will die because life-saving medicine or surgery isn't available in 1631? How do you cope with watching them slowly die from something that was curable, before? Greg Ferrara, Linda Bartolli, and Phillip Bartolli are forced to face these questions when the Ring of Fire happens weeks before Tina was scheduled for lifesaving surgery that, like her life-saving medication, is no longer available.

And what do you do when your wife really wants a bagel with cream cheese but they haven't been invented yet?

https://www.baen.com/gourmets-of-grantville.html

Red Shield

Bethanne Kim

Red Shield

Bethanne Kim

Big battles may be fought with APCs and battleships, but when a small West Virginia town goes back through time and space to land in Thuringia, Germany in 1631, there are bigger battles to fight. Ones the military might struggle with. The kind meant for octogenarians, parents, and teens.

Whether their goal is preserving the past, ensuring the future, or making the world a better place, these volunteers aren't going to accept "it can't be done" as the answer.

Some of their goals may sound simple—teaching hand washing for Pete's sake!—but the missions of the Red Cross and Scouts have never been more important, and their tools more in need of evolving, to win the hearts and minds of the new world that surrounds them than in the 1630s.

No matter what the tool or the fight, Grantvillers are ready for battle and the world better "Be Prepared" for *Stayin' Alive* West Virginia style!

https://www.baen.com/red-shield.html

The Marshalls

Mike Watson

The Marshals

Mike Watson

The New United States is about to join the United States of Europe, becoming the State of Thuringia and Franconia. The Thirty Years' War is still being waged. Armies cross and re-cross the German states. With war comes lawlessness, and with lawlessness comes the need for law and order.

Who can fill this enforcement niche better than three retired old soldiers, known to down-timers as *Die Drei Alten Soldaten?* Archie Mitchell, Harley Thomas, Max Huffman, retired US Army master sergeants who, with their apprentice, Dieter Issler, use their up-time experience as deputy sheriffs to become the first Marshals of the newly created District Court system of the SoTF.

The Marshals are little known until Thomas Bloem and his sister, Maria D'Angelo, brother and sister journalists, arrive to interview them. They record the formation of the Marshal's Service and the three Marshals, from their first case as Marion County Deputy Sheriffs, until they leave Grantville to provide law and order throughout the State of Thuringia and Franconia.

https://www.baen.com/the-marshalls.html

Time Spike: The Mysterious Mesa

Garrett W. Vance

Time Spike: The Mysterious Mesa

Garrett W. Vance

The time-twisting Assiti Shards are the distressing consequences of a highly advanced and completely insane alien race's idea of art. One of the shards has struck in the southern Illinois region, thrusting peoples from different historical eras into the middle of one of the most dangerous periods ever known: The Cretaceous! Lost in a nightmare world, a conquistador from the year 1541 finds a U.S. Cavalry Scout from 1838 hanging helplessly from a snare. The Spaniard frees him, an act of mercy leading to an uneasy alliance. After battling a "dragon" we know as the Tyrannosaurus Rex, they find themselves in the shadows of the Cyclopean pyramids of Cahokia, the greatest city of the forgotten Mississippian civilization. The Rattlesnake Priests prepare a grisly celebration for their reptilian god, but thanks to the intervention of the Raven Priestess, they escape the city with a pair of Pre-Mound tribesmen who invite the castaways from the future to join them in their beleaguered village. They find the villagers trying to defend themselves from the giant creatures roaming this primeval land. Thankfully, a new hope can be seen across the vast, dry flats of the Drained Sea—a mysterious mesa rising more than a thousand feet into the sky, another bizarre result of the unnatural disaster. Could this be a haven? To find out, the four newfound friends set out on a journey that will prove to be more dangerous than anything they have faced yet!

https://www.baen.com/time-spike-the-mysterious-mesa.html

Time Spike: The First Cavalry Of The Cretaceous

Garrett W. Vance

Time Spike: The First Cavalry Of The Cretaceous

Garrett W. Vance

The unlikely foursome of an AWOL US cavalry scout, a repentant conquistador, and two young chiefs of a neolithic pre-mounds tribe have formed a friendship and alliance that breaks the bonds of centuries and cultures. They are now the 'dragon'-slaying four Great Chiefs of the young Mesa Peoples and Allied Tribes, a human civilization growing against steep odds in the Earth's Cretaceous Period (introduced in *Time Spike: The Mysterious Mesa).*

These bold heroes now face a formidable foe, not the enormous dinosaurs that roam this ancient world, but other humans! The rapacious Rattlesnake Cult from the City of the Pyramids has laid siege to Stone Wall Village. Only the newly-minted First Cavalry of the Cretaceous, brave pre-mounds warriors astride a prehistoric equine species native to Pleistocene North America have a chance of saving their kinfolk and restoring peace and prosperity in the lush and deadly *New* New World. Here comes the cavalry!

https://www.baen.com/time-spike-first-cavalry-of-the-cretaceous.htm
l

Saving The Dodo

Garrett W. Vance

Saving the Dodo

Garrett W. Vance

This book is an extensive rewrite and expansion of "Second Chance Bird."

Every American knows about the poor dodo, the veritable poster child of wildlife extinction. When Caroline Platzer explains the bird's total extinction to her young charge, Princess Kristina, the very upset princess is determined to do something about it—and it may not be too late! The last recorded sighting of the dodo was in 1662 and now it is only the year of our lord 1635. Maybe, just maybe . . .

Enter Pam Miller, Grantville's resident birdwatcher and nature lover. When asked by Princess Kristina to lead a mission to the distant Indian Ocean Isle of Mauritius to prevent the hapless dodo's inevitable extinction, Pam agrees. Wasn't saving the dodo one of her own childhood dreams? Now, thanks to the Ring of Fire, maybe she actually can! She and Princess Kristina hatch a plan, bonded by their mutual love for the natural world.

The whole thing will be terribly risky, a long journey in a sailing ship around the Horn of Africa and out into the still mostly unexplored vastness of the Southern Indian Ocean. Can Pam Miller really save the dodo? Can she save herself and her companions from the multitude of threats they will face along the way? The only thing Pam knows for sure is that this is her chance to change history, and an ungainly flightless bird is counting on her.

https://www.baen.com/saving-the-dodo.html

COMING SOON

I Want To Be Your Hero

Kerryn Offord

I Want to Be Your Hero

Kerryn Offord

Coming May 5, 2026

The universe is insistent on making John Felix "Puss" Trelli a hero. He doesn't think he is, or ever could be. Yet every time he winds up in danger, he acts like the hero he thinks he cannot be. From the first pages, where he is attacked by a "mad" dog, he freezes, but the people around him see him as standing between them and the danger. He believes he's given the St.George Medal for Valor under false pretenses, but he goes along with the War Bond tour with his handler, Corporal Svetlana Andreyevna Bergman. When he gets dragooned into taking Sveta to a wedding as her date, the rumors fly that they are an item. Will love blossom between these two? How can it, when Puss is stationed in a variety of foreign places. Can a relationship be made by mail? This exciting novel by the co-author of the Doctor Gribbleflotz books will give you an answer you might not expect.

https://www.baen.com/i-want-to-be-your-hero.html

May 2026 Baen Bundle (dissolves May 5):

https://www.baen.com/w202605-may-2026-monthly-baen-bundle.html

Up-Time Pride And Down-Time Prejudice

Mark Huston

Up-Time Pride, Down-Time Prejudice

Mark Huston

Coming May 5, 2026

In the Year of our Lord 1633, Mary Margret Russo graduates from Grantville High School at the top of her class. The beautiful and strong willed up-timer, as the people from the future are called, is mysteriously hired by a branch of the wealthiest family in the world. Mary finds herself far from her family, living in a beautiful castle in the Inn Valley of Tyrol. There she meets Counts, Countesses, the handsome and distant Count Johann Franz, and works hard as a teacher and consultant among the one-percenters of the day. But all is not what it seems in this gilded world, where religion, undercurrents of witchcraft, and vast sums of money create high-stakes contests, and where treachery and death await the unwary or the unprepared. Can a resolute and intelligent girl find love, happiness, and purpose in this world where she is the ultimate outsider, out of her time, alone, and in dangers she cannot comprehend?

https://www.baen.com/up-time-pride-and-down-time-prejudice-2026.html

May 2026 Baen Bundle (dissolves May 5):

https://www.baen.com/w202605-may-2026-monthly-baen-bundle.html

No Ship For Tranquebar

Kevin H Evans and Karen C Evans

No Ship for Tranquebar

Kevin H. Evans and Karen C. Evans

Coming June 2, 2026

Marlon Pridmore was more than a small-town loan officer. He also loved to tinker and make things—the more difficult, the better. Then, he found himself caught up in the Ring of Fire and flung into the seventeenth century with no hope of return. He decided to ease his frustrations by building his first airship—which he also intended to be his last.

Or so he thought. Mike Stearns, the president of the New United States, had other plans—and so, he discovered, did some gentlemen of the Danish East India Company.

His frustration giving way to excitement, Marlon rose to the challenge. Could he build an airship that would fly from Denmark to India?

https://www.baen.com/no-ship-for-tranquebar-2026.html

June 2026 Baen Bundle:

https://www.baen.com/w202606-june-2026-monthly-baen-bundle.html

Fire On The Rio Grande

Kevin H Evans and Karen C Evans

Fire On The Rio Grande

Kevin H Evans and Karen C Evans

Coming June 2, 2026

It begins with word of a town from the future.

In the Spanish province of Nuevo Mexico, Father Philip, the only Jesuit north of the Rio Grande, receives letters full of information from a new town in Germany full of time travelers. Just one article from the Britannica lights a revolt of the native population.

Eduardo Bernal, born in Nuevo Mexico and just sixteen years old, loves the place of his birth and his native neighbors. Can he save them from Spanish colonial prejudice and religious repression?

Will Nuovo Mexico be the first colony to throw out European governance?

Will it end in the first American Revolution?

https://www.baen.com/fire-on-the-rio-grande-2026.html

June 2026 Baen Bundle:

https://www.baen.com/w202606-june-2026-monthly-baen-bundle.html

1637: The Pilgrim's Passage

Eric Flint and Griffin Barber

1637: The Pilgrim's Passage

Eric Flint and Griffin Barber

Coming August 4, 2026

The Ring of Fire Series Returns with Conflict and Intrigue in the Middle East!

The more things change, the more they stay the same. . . .

Jahanara Begum is on pilgrimage, a journey and rite every Muslim must essay if able. The up-timers of the USE Mission are escorting the princess in her travels to Jeddah before returning home, their mission accomplished and allies made of the court of Dara Shikoh, having helped to place him on the Peacock Throne.

But the pilgrimage is only the public-facing reason for her departure from Agra.

In reality, the begum sahib is also carrying her love child off to Jeddah in hopes of giving birth in secrecy. Everyone outside the Mission and her most loyal followers must be kept ignorant of the impending birth, a feat which would be hard enough if her brother hadn't saddled her with the presence of her great aunt and frequent adversary, the sometime empress Nur Jahan.

If the presence of her most brilliant adversary in her court wasn't enough, a Mughal princess abroad is an important figure, and the political situation in the Hijaz—a complex of relations between Ottoman Bey, Sharif of the Hijaz, the Bedouin, and Persian interests—is about to boil over.

Can Jahanara Begum and her USE allies safely navigate the power politics of the Pilgrim's Passage?

https://www.baen.com/1637-the-pilgrim-s-passage.html

August 2026 Baen Bundle

https://www.baen.com/w202608-august-2026-monthly-baen-bundle.html

Supporting the 1632verse

We appreciate our readers, and we thank you for continuing to support the 1632 universe. None of the things in this section are likely to be news to most of our readers, but here are some ways you can support us more.

Reviews

This is pretty straight-forward: Books that have more reviews (especially positive ones) are promoted more, so we need our readers to review our books.

So pretty please and thank you, take a minute to review this book. And if you leave a comment in addition to stars, know that we will read it and we appreciate the time you take for those comments!

Give a 1632 Gift

1632 is a free download from Baen. Issue 1 of Eric Flint's 1632 & Beyond is a free download on 1632Magazine.com and Baen. Please share them with anyone you think might get hooked!

You can give (or receive) a gift subscription to 1632 & Beyond. Just choose "gift" when you add it to your cart.

We also have some branded items available to buy on our Zazzle store. There is a coffee mug with the Hangman Regiment logo, an Apple watch band with a becky (currency), and a wine bottle tote with the cover from Issue 2. We hope you find something fun you enjoy! If you have a suggestion for something new, just let us know and there's a good chance we'll add it.

https://www.zazzle.com/store/1632_and_beyond

Buy Another Issue

There are 102 volumes of the Grantville Gazette and a new issue of 1632 & Beyond every other month. That's a lot! Have you read them all? If not, bundles of six (one year of the magazine) are a great way to save some money. They are priced at six for the cost of five.

Buy a 1632 Baen Novel

The Grantville Gazette and now Eric Flint's 1632 & Beyond are the short story venues for the 1632verse and Baen publishes the novels. While we (obviously) benefit more directly from magazine purchases, we still benefit indirectly when you buy novels from Baen. Some of us also benefit directly as authors receiving royalties.

The Baen books fall roughly into two camps right now. First, the mainline novels. These are generally the ones released in hardback and then paperback in addition to ebooks. (Again, roughly speaking.) Then there are the ebook only releases. As of 2026, the majority of these were originally published by Ring of Fire Press, but there are two fully new novels (*Security Solutions* by Bjorn Hasseler and *Red Shield* by Bethanne Kim). Baen has provided new covers and polished all the former RoFP novels a bit more before re-releasing them.

There are dozens of mainline books from Baen. The link below lists them all by publication date. There are also links to a list chronological within the universe and one by storyline.

https://author.1632magazine.com/canon-continuity/1632-books-by-publication-date/

Connect with us on Social Media

We would love to hear from you here at *Eric Flint's 1632 & Beyond!* There are lots of ways to get in touch with us and we look forward to hearing from you.

Main Sites

Email: 1632Magazine@1632Magazine.com

Shop: 1632Magazine.com

Author Site: Author.1632Magazine.com

For anyone interested in writing in the 1632verse, or fans interested in more background on the series and how we keep track of everything.

Facebook

Our Facebook Group is our primary social media, but we do use the FB Page, YouTube, and Flickr accounts.

Facebook Group: The Grantville Gazette / 1632 & Beyond

We also have a Facebook Page at Facebook.com/t1632andBeyond.

YouTube

We have quite a lot on our YouTube Channel because we have videos of most of the panels from at least four separate 1632 Minicons, including FenCon in 2025, FantaSci in 2024, and several with Eric and other now-deceased authors on the panels. In addition, we have playlists with videos of Mannington, the town Grantville was based on. We know we have an international readership, so one of the playlists shows real estate listings for typical Mannington homes, to give y'all a more realistic idea of what they really look like.

YouTube: 1632andBeyond

Flickr

These images are mostly of Mannington, WV, the town Grantville is based on. There are a lot more ranchers, trailers, and other humble, normal homes than this may lead you to expect because, well, it's more fun to share photos of a freshly remodeled painted lady than a double-wide with a pickup and two ATVs in the yard.

https://www.flickr.com/photos/199556693@N05/albums

Reviews and More

You are welcome to join us on **BaensBar.net**. Most of the chatting about 1632 on the Bar is in the 1632 Tech forum. If you want to read and comment on possible future stories, check out 1632 Slush (stories) and 1632 Slush Comments on BaensBar.net.

Last but far from least, if you are interested in writing in the 1632 universe, that's fabulous! Please visit **Author.1632Magazine.com** (QR code) for more information.

Circling back to the very first way to help: Reviews really matter, especially for small publishers and indie authors, so please take a few minutes to post a review online or wherever you find books, and don't forget to tell your friends to check us out!

www.ingramcontent.com/pod-product-compliance
Lightning Source LLC
LaVergne TN
LVHW010653110826
845149LV00014B/3064

9781962398381